Murder, Scandal and Cliches

Written by John Threlkeld
Book cover designed by Cally Devonport

Murder, Scandal and Cliches

Dedicated to Cally Mae, Charly Devonport and Alfred Barker, who knew of the existence of the secret military tunnels in his hometown of Wombwell and inspired the novel.

Murder, Scandal and Cliches

Chapter 1
The year, 1942

THE influence eccentric Mary Elliott wielded over the village of Gorton in wartime Britain was a strange affair. Even the local policeman, known as Bobby Lee, did not ask too many questions about the activities of the mysterious lady living in the big house, Two Trees.

Known as Lady Bountiful, she generously funded the construction of the sturdy scout hut, the pride of Gorton (population 4, 000) and supplied free uniforms to all the scouts and girl guides. At Christmas she paid for hot festive meals and drinks for 40 or so retired miners and their families.

She was held in high esteem as the newspaper, the Northfield Advertiser, based in the neighbouring large town (population: 200,000), stated in its columns on frequent occasions.

The middle-aged spinster was executive secretary of the Northfield Main Mining Company in south Yorkshire, a large operation employing 2,000 men, and was regarded by many as the unofficial lady of the manor.

A perceptive resident told a neighbour one day: "Where does all the money come from? She must have an ample salary but surely she can't afford all the good deeds. What do you think? Look at the size of that house. Look at the beautiful grounds."

The surreptitious conversations in back yards and the main street never really evolved into anything more than a few sharp retorts and questions. For most people felt in a peculiar way that criticising 'Our Mary' was akin to severe disloyalty to one of their own. Perhaps she was loaded but she was born and brought up in Gorton.

Others did not want to tarnish the character of the local worthy and magistrate. Strangers to the village were politely excluded from joining in conversations about her since controversial parish pump talk was not encouraged to be spread beyond its boundary marker.

On a bleak Saturday in the winter of 1942, she was driving her Daimler on a routine tour of the village. That's when she saw P.c Lee walking along the main street on his way to collect witness statements after a nasty scrummage in the tap room of The Albion Inn the previous night. In addition, there was a report of stolen milk bottles from doorsteps on the council estate and he couldn't forget little Jimmy, a seven-year-old who regarded the policeman as his colossus.

Halting the car a few feet from the approaching policeman, she wound down the window: "Oh, P.c Lee. How's your wife and boy? Are they well? I believe Susan has had a heavy cold; I do hope she gets better soon.

"Oh, please don't take too much notice if you see any builders' wagons and workmen on my drive this afternoon. Just having a few jobs done. Nothing spectacular, you understand. It's all hush hush. Secret service and all that."

"What do you mean..hush hush?" he asked, suspiciously.

"Oh, nothing like that! No. No. It's just my phraseology. I have been listening to too many spy dramas on the wireless. More enjoyable than Tommy Handley and his ITMA comedy programme, don't you think? I am just making my house ship shape, but I do not want too many people to know what I am doing. That's all."

P.c Lee, a suave man with a rich mop of blond hair, looked like the latest Hollywood film idol, William Holden, Mary concluded; not too rugged and not too soft featured. She couldn't help wondering whether there was a mistress tucked away in one of the terraced streets. According to her wild imagination all good -looking men had a tart on the side; she had seen a few of his predecessors earn themselves stellar reputations as lady killers before being hurriedly transferred to posts elsewhere.

At any rate, she thought his wife was frumpish and that was a good reason for a man to wander from the marital bed. Not that Mary had any romantic intentions since she was in her mid- 40s, and all that kind of thing was securely locked away in her past.

"Fine. Okay, Miss Elliott," replied the officer before heading for a rendezvous with little Jimmy who was standing on a street corner.

"Hello, Mr Lee, want to hear my joke?"

"Go on Jimmy, can't wait."

"Why does Mr Churchill take a gun to bed?"

"No idea, Jimmy," replied P.c Lee, who had heard it many times but as a patient man with children did not let on. "Go on, tell me."

"Because there is a jerry (chamber pot; wartime slang for a German) under the bed."

P.c Lee shook with laughter, though he doubted whether the lad knew what a jerry was, while Jimmy thought he had the golden touch with jokes-of-the-week.

"Oh, Jimmy, can you pass on a message to your father? Please say I'll meet him tonight at 8pm. He knows what it's all about. Now you do not forget, it's important. You'll be in trouble if you do. A night in the cells if you are not careful."

Having thanked the lad for sharing his humour, the officer walked on and collected the statements regarding the pub fight, which absorbed most of the morning. In the bar the landlord was told there was one other task to carry out before heading home to prepare his reports. Then he walked out of The Albion and was not seen again. He disappeared.

Where was he heading? No one seemed to know. The police sergeant at the principal police station in Northfield had no idea where he was, and the officer's wife was nonplussed. She had a sneaky feeling another woman was involved since he had a wandering eye, but she had never been able to produce firm evidence after the suspicions were planted in her head by gossips.

After a few hours the police poured into the village, searching fields and woodland and the homes of criminals who may have had a grudge. Gardens were dug up and hundreds of people interviewed. There were no signs of him.

The mystery monopolised the front pages of the Advertiser for a month until one week a gruesome murder of a girl at the fairground in Northfield became the predominant story, and residents began to push Bobby Lee into the back of their minds.

In the absence of facts rumours began to circulate. He had run away with Mrs So-and-So who had left for London the day before his disappearance, though police enquiries proved there was no truth in that one. Then there was an outlandish rumour he had been kidnapped by German spies and spirited away to the Fatherland, yet no-one offered an explanation as to why they wanted to conduct such a daring operation on a man from their village.

The following Saturday Jimmy waited at their meeting place. He lounged around for ten minutes convinced his hero would turn up and prove the rest of the villagers wrong. Then he went home alone, shaking his head and with tears on his cheeks.

A few streets away from Jimmy's home was the terraced house where Mark Pinder, a miner and a union branch official at the pit, was sitting at the kitchen table, having finished the morning shift. His face and hands were still blackened with grime and pit dust, for he insisted on having his hot meal before his wife, Doris, scrubbed him down in the tin bath in front of the blazing coal fire.

Doris placed his meal on the table while Mark's eyes narrowed on spotting a headline on the front page of the Sheffield Star, an evening newspaper which had just been delivered to his home by the newspaper boy. It wasn't the news about the latest German bombing raid on the steel city that caught his attention: P.c Lee's vanishing act continued to dominate the attention of reporters.

"How can a man like him disappear?" a bemused Mark told his wife, who wasn't listening. She was preparing meals for the kids in the never -ending drudgery of keeping on top of cleaning, washing and cooking in the home, the lot of a miner's wife in the 1940s.

"Why hasn't he been found? By now a body should have been discovered. No-one saw him after passing Billy's Hill. There are no houses around there except Two Trees and then it's Hobson's Farm half a mile away. The labourers were in the farm- yard at the time and they did not see him. Couldn't miss him, could you? Not in that uniform.

"An old guy once disappeared down our mine. Years and years ago. He was checked in by the men on the surface. Finished part of a shift hewing coal then vanished. They reckon he made his way into old workings and may have been gassed. No-one saw him again.

"This case is different. Charlie Dickens at the pit says he saw the policeman walking towards the railway station dressed as a tramp. That can't be true. Charlie must have had too much to drink at The Albion. But what happened?"

The P.c. Lee story remained buried in the Advertiser's decaying paper files until the 1960s when Two Trees and the discovery of an underground military bunker left behind by the war made the headlines.

Chapter 2

The year, 1965

Ralph Baines, an ace reporter in his dreams and at the age of 19 the youngest in the Advertiser office, was fascinated by the sight of his boss. Chief reporter Don Smith was reading aloud a newly delivered letter, the contents of which did not interest Ralph, but the cigarette stuck on the reader's bottom lip did. The blue smoke from the cheap Woodbine curled upwards in ever decreasing circles and the white ash at the tip of the cig grew longer and more fragile as he warbled on.

Would it, or wouldn't it? The animated young reporter was using hand signals and winks to communicate with his pal sitting behind Don; both were waiting for the ash to disintegrate and dust the boss's charcoal grey suit, which like the owner had seen better days.

"This looks interesting," declared Don, apparently oblivious to the sneaky goings-on. Sitting motionless and inhaling infrequently, he continued: "It's from the new owners of that big house near Billy's Hill. They have asked the council and the police to have a gander at something they have found in the cellar, and they want us to go along as well.

"I'll ask Phil to cover the story and, Ralph, you can go along for experience. Grab a photographer on your way out of the office."

Don was in his late 40s, had a slight stoop and drawn face, courtesy of too many Woodbine cigarettes, and was proud of his full head of Brylcreemed black hair. New recruits soon realised he was the real boss in the office despite the presence of an Editor. On good days he was known as The Guru; when things went wrong the staff were less respectful.

To Ralph's dismay Don suddenly flicked away the cig ash and stubbed the tab in the tray. The lad, for once, had miscalculated and lost his bet that the ash would remain perched at the tip of the cig for another three seconds. His face drooped: the ash had failed to perform its anticipated and untouched-by-fingers collapse from the lips.

"Two Trees, "mused Don. "That's the house where mad Mary Elliott lived during the war. God she was a woman. So petite, so nice and so deceitful. Perhaps evil."

"Who was she?" replied Ralph, trying to drum up enthusiasm for another assignment that promised to be as woefully boring as the one that failed to occupy his attention the previous day.

Don, now reminiscing and therefore smiling for the first time that day, sparked into life: "She was rich and appeared to be respectable. Pillar of the establishment and a magistrate. She was also

13

company secretary of the local mining company."

Ralph interrupted him: "What happened? What did she do wrong? Dad talked about a scandal years ago, but I did not take much notice in those days."

His boss fired back: "I am not telling. It's your job to find out. I won't hand out things on a plate. Anyway, this invitation may have nothing to do with Elliott. Just find out what they have discovered. It's something to do with a secret tunnel. At least it will be read on publication day, making a change from your turgid golden wedding anniversary reports and church news."

For a moment Ralph thought his boss knew what went on behind his back on slow and smoky news days and that the last comment was his nasty response to having been the office joke for two minutes. Not that he had to worry since Don was just being irascible due to middle age.

The news team travelled to Two Trees in typical local newspaper style. The old Morris saloon, like a certain charcoal grey suit, had seen better days and all three occupants felt every bump in the road as it sped from the main office in Church Street, Northfield.

The driver, Phil, who was in his early 20s, was ambitious with his eye on a better paid job in the Sheffield Star's newspaper branch office in Northfield, believing the latest assignment would bolster his chances. The car, having exerted itself on the way, wheezed up the curved drive to halt in front of the house on the hill.

Chapter 3

"That's some pad," Ralph announced to his pals in the car as he eyed Two Trees, the mock Tudor-style house built by Miss Elliott at the peak of the depression in the 1930s.

"I have not seen it up so close before; I have always been on the other side of the gates. To a lad the house had an air of grandeur and mystery about it."

"You must have had an overripe imagination," muttered Phil, a lean six-footer known as the man who deflated dreams and who had an eye for the ladies.

The distinctive half-timbered frame, the steeply pitched roof and arched front door reminded Ralph of film stars and glamorous lives, and as they approached the owner standing in the drive he wondered what the full story behind Miss Elliott and the house was.

His boss knew about her dark life, particularly the court case, but kept most of the details to himself as if he owned the copyright.

Her story was fascinating. During the 1930s Miss Elliott, who was not interested in marriage, poured her energy into the job of helping to run the local colliery, and she made sure that her home reflected her growing status in Gorton and Northfield.

The house was beautifully presented with commodious rooms downstairs, where lavish parties and dinners were held for the benefit of the landed gentry, civic leaders, and the chief constable before the war. There were six bedrooms and two bathrooms and the locals who waged a daily and losing battle against soot in the air and coal dust on bodies marvelled at the thought that a local house could have two gleaming baths.

"Too much money, that's her trouble," a miner's wife said wearily on being told the unfounded rumour that the bathroom taps were gold-plated, simultaneously eyeing with disdain the tin bath hanging on a nail in the kitchen. "Even some of the Hollywood stars do not have taps that expensive."

Lady Bountiful adored the place, spending her spare time before the war searching for quality furniture in London and tasteful chandeliers and wallpaper from abroad, the cost of which raised snooty eyebrows in dining rooms across the county. Her response to inquisitive friends was always the same: "My grandfather had properties in Scotland and left his darling princess a fortune. I am a lucky lady."

The opulent house became a focal point for locals. Families out walking halted outside the double metal gates and peered at the frontage, noting for example the leaded windows that were said to have been bought from a rundown country house in Derbyshire

Their undivided attention was drawn to the neatly laid out gardens, the miniature scenic railway that was built for the benefit of children and to the two oak trees sited on either side of the drive, and after which the house was named.

"Some people have all the luck," was often heard as the pedestrians made their way home to their modest terraced house or council home, though there was that nagging doubt that there was something wrong with the set-up at the house. However, the no grassing culture embedded in mining communities always prevailed. It was nothing to do with anyone outside Gorton - not even in the neighbouring town of Northfield.

As well as being a company secretary she was a JP at the borough magistrates' court, handing out penalties and fines to petty criminals and a much sought after public speaker on the local circuit, addressing women's groups and the church fellowship.

Her favourite topic: a motoring holiday to Bavaria in Nazi Germany in 1937. Returning from Germany in a jubilant mood and having concluded the country was highly efficient and prosperous, she believed it was the template for the future of Western Civilisation.

Audiences found her views on Adolf Hitler persuasive, and she was thrilled when the newspaper asked for an interview, though the resulting article applauding the achievements of the Fascist state was viciously attacked by the local miners' union. The principal critic was Mark Pinder, senior, the union firebrand.

Bruised by the attacks and unable to comprehend why anyone would find her views worthy of such a reaction, she became reclusive, turning her attention again to her first love, Two Trees. The library of leather-bound books was reorganised and the beloved garden redesigned, her gardeners planting a barrier of pine trees to shield her fiefdom from the prying eyes beyond the double gates.

With close friends worrying about the state of her mental health, a second screen of trees was planted at the rear of the house, not far from open fields where she claimed shadowy figures were beginning to appear, fuelling her paranoia when alone at night

Most of the public thought the house was a marvel, but there was one conspicuous feature that went unnoticed even by the nosiest of observers. It was larger and more extensively furnished than the house owned by the company's managing director 20 miles away, an anomaly that should have set the alarm bells ringing not only in the colliery offices but in the police station.

The managing director, George Burton, the great grandson of the self-made man who financed the sinking of the shafts at the pit in 1858, was well-educated, an aloof character who spent little time at the colliery. He did not socialise with staff and never visited Two Trees despite being told by his secretary that it was 'a little palace.'

The establishment developed a curious blind spot towards Mary. The police, for example, thought anyone of her status, sweetness and dottiness was incapable of doing anything wrong. That attitude was shattered when there was a chance meeting between Burton and the managing director of the company's bank in London. Burton thought the pit was making a profit; the bank chief contradicted him by saying it was making substantial losses.

The police were called in and Mary, aged 47, was charged with fraud and embezzlement – she had kept two sets of accounts and books, one for the benefit of the company directors and the other for the bank– and at Leeds Assizes in 1944 she was sentenced to six years of penal servitude.

She had robbed the company of £100,000 – the equivalent of £5 ½ million today – but at least half of the village felt sorry for her. Graffiti appeared on walls and railway bridges criticising the hard-line judiciary and declaring her punishment was disgraceful.

Don Smith, then a young court reporter, never forgot the unconventional reaction from the village to the prison sentence - it seemed out of step in an otherwise deferential community.

Particularly as he had listened to representatives of the law addressing the court, including the prosecuting counsel: "Two Trees was an ideal home for a Lady of the Manor. In Miss Elliott's case she thought she was a Lady, but she was really a charlatan and a fraud." Her own counsel admitted: "She is guilty but mad."

The public read the long accounts of the case in the national newspapers and were stunned to learn from police and a medical expert that she had a mind that was much sharper than that of the criminals she punished at the magistrates' court.

It was finally noted that she had never taken a day off or went on holiday a few weeks before the arrival of the outside auditors, though there was a rumour one or two of them knew what was going off and were paid handsomely by her to keep their mouths shut.

Following the court case, the house and contents was auctioned off to compensate the company. The Advertiser went to town on that memorable day, filling its pages with photographs of the auctioneer, the lots, dealers and scores of curious locals attending the event of the year in Gorton. Many were more interested in seeing what the interior of the big house was like than spending money.

Not that the villagers could have afforded the prices. A George 1 walnut wing armchair with floral upholstery realised £300 (today's valuation: £15,000) and a George 111 inlaid satinwood and painted Pembroke table £350, and they were just two of the lots published in the auctioneer's catalogue.

The wordy feature accompanying the illustrations in the newspaper omitted to reveal she was a former 'esteemed member of the community.'

On her departure the house exchanged hands numerous times over a few years but later became rundown, and a pair of owls took over a bedroom for a period. That led to eerie noises: several revellers joked that Mary and her imaginary creatures returned at night to play tricks on them. The stories became part of folklore and generations of residents sustained her memory by repeating them to their children, a double-edged ploy that helped to inform and give them a brief but healthy scare at bedtime.

By the early 1960s, in the wake of the Conservative Government's 'never had it so good' boom, expensive houses became fashionable again for the middle classes and a series of doctors followed each other into Two Trees. In 1964 Dr Paul Potter and his wife were the owners when a secret military complex was discovered during a refurbishment.

Chapter 4

Unaware that their routine lives were poised to be upended, the two intrepid reporters and the photographer were taken indoors by Dr Potter. The wide stone steps at the front of the house swept to a solid oak oversized front door and to a solid oak floor in the reception hall, with a gently curving staircase in the background. The trio bypassed the ground floor rooms and were escorted down a long flight of cold stone steps leading into a spacious cellar, part of which had been used as an air-raid shelter during the war, with personalised alcoves for Mary's pet dogs.

"I take it you know all about Miss Elliott?" asked Dr Potter, as the group walked around what Ralph thought was a quite forbidding place, like a dungeon. "Quite a lady."

"Oh yes, we all know about her," replied Phi, glibly. "We have an ancient oracle in the office who witnessed what happened in the dark ages."

Dr Potter gave him a peculiar look as he was not party to office politics but ignoring the remark said they were awaiting the team from the police and the council, then everyone would be shown the secret door.

"Sounds intriguing," added Phil, now becoming excited at the thought of something that was more riveting than routine court cases involving drunks. Ralph, however, remained subdued, having been convinced that life in Northfield was permanently dull.

Once the full group had assembled in the cellar the host produced a large key and moved an old wooden cabinet hugging the wall, revealing a steel door. It was ultra- solid, polished and looked bomb-proof, like something at the entrance to the vaults of a bank.

Ralph, a student of bad black-and-white thrillers at the local cinema, suddenly became absorbed in what was unfolding, recalling a scene in an Edgar Wallace Mystery Theatre film in which a gang broke into a bank by tunnelling into its vaults via an empty shop next door. The doctor inserted the key and with a hefty push the door shuddered and opened, a motley collection of rust, dust and cobwebs falling from the hinges. There was also an overriding odour of decay.

"As you can see, gentlemen, it's a tunnel and not a coal mine," said the doctor. "Oh, I have forgotten the illumination. We found this tunnel, sorry a network of tunnels, three months ago and I got the local electrician to rig-up a new electricity supply and spotlights so we could find out what this is all about. This 'find', never mentioned by the estate agent selling the house, has generated a lot of interest in the family and we wanted to share our enthusiasm with the outside world."

A switch was flicked and a shaft of light from a spotlight flooded the passageway for about 50 yards ahead, revealing walls and a ceiling dripping with water that until recently had not been seen for 20 years. Ralph, his nostrils twitching as a blast of foul air rushed out of the darkness, reached for his handkerchief.

"Good God," he told another member of the group, "I hope there is no methane gas here: the old files of my newspaper are stuffed with horrific stories about explosions that killed thousands of men, women and children at mines over a couple of centuries."

Smiling weakly, the officer from the council pretended to ignore him and continued to make notes, wondering why the scribes were not doing the same.

As Ralph's eyes grew accustomed to the light, he could see that the tunnel was about eight foot high and six ft foot wide. Even to his untrained mind he realised it had been skilfully hewed out of the rock beneath the house, the men, whoever they were, having done a better job than the squads of tough professionals who had excavated the underground galleries at local pits.

"Who was behind all this?" he wondered as the party made its way into the now fascinating underworld. Again his mind turned to gas, a miner's deadliest enemy. He hoped the ventilation system was working and he chuckled at the thought that had Don, the inveterate smoker, been there, and had there been methane gas, the complex would be a smoking ruin.

After another 20-yard trek the doctor turned his torch on a small box attached to the wall and flicked another switch, the light swallowing a further 10 yards of darkness in front of them. A couple of minutes later the party, now struggling with the humidity and dust in the depths of the complex, came across another door, a structure which had once been solid enough to withstand an explosion caused by a grenade or small bomb. It was now showing its age and as evidence the doctor pointed to rotting fragments of wood that were littering the floor.

Ralph thought the general practitioner ought to have been a thespian or a showman in a circus. With a flourish of his hands and beaming at his nonplussed new friends, the doctor declared: "We are now at the epicentre of our discovery, what we think is marvel from the second world war."

The door was opened, beyond which was a spacious room complete with old chairs, a table and beds and beyond that another room with wash basins, toilets and a primitive shower unit. Large wooden cupboards were leaning haphazardly against the walls. What had been stored there? Rifles, revolvers, Bren guns, ammunition and explosives?

"This is it," concluded the host. "We believe this is a second world war military bunker where our lads would have made a last stand against the enemy. Shades of Winston Churchill and fighting on the beaches.

"Beyond this room there is another long tunnel which may have been used by the defenders had the German insurgents managed to break into the interior. It leads into the garden rockery where there is a once hidden exit; we had to remove a few ornamental stones, a bird bath and huge amounts of soil to get to it from the outside. The long tunnel has a series of bends behind which we believe the retreating soldiers would have hidden for a few minutes, picking off the enemy before fleeing via the exit into the garden and hopefully to freedom."

"Doctor, what's all this about?" asked Phil, who was flummoxed, for he was no student of the military or the war.

"That's why you and the other gentlemen are here," stressed the doctor. "Obviously it's something to do with the war. Not sure about the details; some of what has been said is speculation.

"It must have been very unusual for the military to have constructed an underground and superbly fitted out bunker in a small village on the outskirts of a large town. Perhaps the house, given its size and strategic position on a hillside, would have been commandeered by the army in the event of an invasion. It would have made a perfect regimental headquarters and had things got stickier the elite would have moved underground. However, that's a theory at this stage."

Phil asked: "What were all those manhole covers in the ceiling of one of the tunnels? They looked strange."

Replying, the doctor said: "We think they were escape hatches. You could open them only from the inside. Everything was so carefully worked out, but it all turned out to be a waste of time. There was no invasion."

The doctor said it was for someone else to finish off enquiries. He was convinced there was a dusty file languishing somewhere in a cabinet in Whitehall that would explain everything. The reporters finally began taking notes and interviewed the doctor and his wife, asking how they had found the bunker and persuading them to elaborate on their theories.

The council official who had been scribbling notes earlier was now pleased the Advertiser men were doing the same, in effect doing their job rather than merely listening.

What the man from the town hall did not realise was that experience had taught Phil, now a fully trained reporter, that minimising note taking enabled him to concentrate on the important aspects of the story such as what the doctor was revealing. Too much information and too many spidery shorthand outlines on a page of his notebook fogged the mind while typing at speed.

"Where were the keys to the bunker?" asked Phil.

"They were left in a cardboard box in the cellar by the previous owner. There was no note of explanation. We came across them by chance after finding the main entrance to the tunnels."

The photographer reconnoitred the network of

underground rooms and galleries, taking pictures and muttering all the time about the musty air, the dirt, the spiders, and other creepy crawlies that seemed to have found a subterranean paradise. Photographers on weekly newspapers were known as a moaning breed and Sid was no exception.

The two police officers made notes and the men from the Northfield town hall began preparing a report which would find its way to the borough council's general purposes committee, after which it would be perused by the council's Labour leader and the town clerk. Then, following further vetting by the 56 councillors, it would be forwarded to Whitehall where it would be temporarily lost in a labyrinth of offices and corridors before resurfacing on a minister's overladen desk.

M.I 5. was much more efficient and quicker off the mark than the men from the town hall. A week after publication and before the council's bulky file had set off on its tortuous journey along the corridors of power in London, a spy catcher and a man from the Ministry arrived at the offices of the humble Advertiser.

The Editor, Ronald Yates, was impressed and quite excited by the impending arrival of such important men. It made a change from Randolph Octavius Denton, an elderly member of the local landed gentry, who visited the office every week to try to persuade the boss to publish his turgid poetry. It never appeared in the columns and Ron had run out of excuses months ago, but Randy would not stay away.

Ron had received a garbled phone call from a pal at the town hall who said the men in trench coats were on their way and that the recent publication of the feature about the riddle of Two Trees may have breached the Official Secrets Act.

"Do not be daft," Ron told his pal, but he was still somewhat pensive when the men from London walked into his office. Not a trench coat in sight: they looked like prosperous bank managers in pin-striped suits and trilbies.

The duo grinned in unison and Ron relaxed. Once the preliminaries were over the men said there was nothing to worry about since the bunker was a relic from the war. Had it been a cold war nuclear complex designed to withstand Russian medium range missiles, then there would be trouble and threats of imprisonment, with the Editor being top of the list of suspects.

It was pointed out to him that the personnel using the Gorton bunker in the war would have been part of the so-called Churchill's Secret Army, a force of highly motivated soldiers set up to sabotage the rear-guard of the German army had England been overrun. The human moles would have harassed supply lines and destroyed factories and coal mines until they were inevitably caught and eliminated by the enemy.

The bunker and its occupants were not anticipated to survive long, according to experts. Life expectancy was said to be like that of a fighter pilot in the first world war – two weeks. To try to enable the soldiers to survive longer than the worst predictions of the War Ministry, and to make sure the Germans did not seize secret information, no official records were retained anywhere, not even in Whitehall.

Unknown to the rest of the underground squad, the officer- in- charge was under orders to kill any outsider who knew of the bunker's existence. The local vicar, for example, may well have been shot on the steps of his church as soon as the Panzers moved into Yorkshire.

The executions would have been required, according to the military, because local middle-class luminaries were used in the early stages of planning the bunker, vetting the backgrounds and characters of any villagers recruited to join the other 14 guerrillas. No criminals or men with flawed characters were permitted to go underground for the duration save for a poacher carefully chosen to help the soldiers live off the land.

One of the secret service men said: "Several of the local VIPs would have known the location of the bunker. Probably they were sworn to secrecy, but the officer-in-charge would not have taken any chances. Secrecy was of paramount importance."

Chapter 5

Later, when Ron the Editor mentioned to his editorial staff that names on the death list may well have included the local vicar, the school headmaster and village policeman, Don the oracle turned serious, harvesting his long memory.

"That's odd," he said. "There was a village policeman who disappeared near Two Trees during the war and was never traced. Just vanished as in a magician's trick. If that kind of thing happened these days, newspapers would speculate that aliens had abducted him. In those days we just accepted it after a few weeks and thought he had run off with a woman."

The other reporters, who were typing or drinking mugs of tea, stopped and looked in his direction but they were not enamoured by his announcement, believing that it was one of his silly stories and reluctantly went back to work.

Don tried to attract his staff's undivided attention again by announcing: "Perhaps the Army killed the policeman to save them the trouble once the Germans arrived," but it was not a good day, and Don was not the office guru. The joke fell flat, and the reporters continued to work, heads bowed over typewriters.

Life in the office, having been disrupted by the men from London, went back to normal. Reporters hammered out news on their ageing typewriters, the solid Bakelite phones never stopped ringing, wastepaper baskets overflowed with crumpled sheets of copy paper, and everyone moaned about the unsightly naked light bulbs hanging from cords attached to the ceiling.

One day they would be replaced with strip lighting, management had eagerly promised months earlier, but nothing was done. The badly worn oilcloth on the floor was another source of irritation among staff.

"When are we going to get carpets?" groaned Joan Draper, a newcomer, and an attractive woman in her early 20s with long silky black hair, high cheekbones, and questioning eyes. She was always immaculately dressed thanks to a generous allowance from her father and rarely came to work in the same clothes twice. She was the daughter of a local businessman and industrialist, had been to finishing school in Switzerland and believed the Advertiser was the dungeon of the publishing world.

"Do not send her into any boozy taprooms at lunchtimes to interview miners on the reasons why the weather this summer is so bloody awful," the Editor told Don on the day she was recruited some weeks earlier. "They'll take her for a ride. They will blame the testing of atomic bombs before 1963 and then have a laugh at our expense on publication day.

"The world is obsessed with radiation and that deadly stuff that gets into milk, Strontium -90. Not that she will know much about that kind of thing. She's a bit sensitive and would have been better off working on a provincial newspaper down south. More suited to the county class and horse riding."

Don gave the Editor a cynical look: "So why did we take her on?"

"We are short of staff. She's keen, wants experience to further her career and dad is a member of my Rotary Club."

Don glanced knowingly at the line of smirking faces in the office before eyeballing the boss: "Nothing to do with that shiny limousine you supposedly hired for your holidays at Scarborough?"

The Editor stormed out of the room, cursing under his breath what he called the jackals in the office and vowing never to speak to Don again.

Life in the office rumbled along until a few days after the underground tour of Two Trees the phone on Don's old desk rang. News from the caller streamed into his ear, setting off mental alarm bells that prompted his eyes to scan the newsroom searching for an experienced reporter and photographer.

The owner of Two Trees was having a nervous breakdown at the other end of the line: what appeared to be the entire borough police force was swarming around his cellar and the tunnels.

"I wish I had never set this stupid enterprise in motion," he fumed. "Police are over the place. You'll have to come and see me."

"What's happened?" asked an exasperated Don. "Have the Russians landed in Northfield? Or have they found old Bobby Lee?"

The last comment was supposed to be another of his barmy jokes since the chances of that happening must have been a million to one.

"How do you know that?" replied the doctor. "Have the police been tipping you off? This is outrageous, wait until I see my MP."

"Crickey," uttered Don, bewildered for once. Was the doctor mad or was he telling the truth?

"Just send those reporters and photographer who came over last week so I can have my say. You don't know what the police will state in public. I'll probably get charged with a murder."

Don put down the receiver and grinned at Phil: "Something big has happened, so find Ralph and the photographer and get over to Two Trees as fast as possible."

The office veteran, whom the rest of the staff thought was terminally past it until requiring a slice of his knowledge, was quite pleased with himself.

"I never thought I could peer into the future," he chuckled. "That doctor will never believe I knew nothing about what was found underground before his phone call."

Then he went back to typing his weekly column which often dealt with dry news from the town hall and drier news from the minutes of water board meetings.

(To boost Don's image among the readership the

Editor had insisted that the illustration accompanying his words in what was called The Onlooker column was that of a silhouette of a young man smoking a pipe rather than a cheap Woodbine. An image of the impressive town hall dominated the background of the illustration to give the impression the writer knew what the local burghers were planning at their secret meetings).

"Well," the doctor announced at Two Trees, "am I glad to see you three. Better not go anywhere near that blasted cellar since it's a crime scene and the constabulary won't even allow me to venture there."

It transpired the doctor harboured bizarre plans to turn part of his old bunker into a wine cellar and drinking saloon for his pals. On removing the old wooden floor in the principal room, the workmen came across a skeleton. Not any man of course but the missing policeman. Tests on a piece of cloth, the remains of his uniform, confirmed that it was the type used by the force 25 years' earlier. To add to the mystery there was a neat bullet hole in the skull.

The doctor asked: "This has nothing to do with us. Miss Elliott lived in this house in those days. Did that little lady kill him? Wasn't there talk of an affair? Can't have been her. A fraudster? Yes! A killer? No. Who was this village policeman?"

Phil's opinion of Don the oracle's journalistic qualities and the breadth of his memory had risen sharply since the revelation he had the added skills of a fortune-teller. With growing confidence, he outlined to the palpably impressed doctor the biography of Bobby Lee and his subsequent Houdini-like act, going into a lot of detail and giving the impression he rather than his boss had unearthed the facts.

"You know your job, don't you?" said the doctor, obviously impressed with the account of what happened during the war. Phil sat back in the armchair bloated with pride while Ralph wondered why Don had briefed his pal rather than him. He was deeply disappointed.

Don waited eagerly for their return. At his age he was more comfortable with what happened in the past than with all the modern gibberish that appeared on his black-and-while television set back home. Elvis Presley and Cliff Richard and their ear-piercing music were beyond his comprehension and the news programmes were seen as superficial.

There was nothing better than a good chinwag about the days when the black market and criminal gangs flourished under the surface in wartime Northfield, he had confided to the managing director a few weeks earlier.

"Well, what happened? Have they found Bobby?" he asked Phil. "I have been thinking about him since you left and there are aspects of the case that I'll be able to help you with. I do not have to go down into our office cellar and comb through those musty newspaper files to find out what happened during the war. My memories are still sound."

Phil outlined what he knew and then settled down behind his typewriter. Placing a cigarette in his mouth, much to the annoyance of the new female journalist who thought smoking was reserved for cocktail bars, he clattered away on the heavy metal keys in frenzied pursuit of clarity and accuracy, which he knew would sap every bit of his mental energy.

He was so preoccupied with the biggest story of the year that he didn't even bother to strike a match, and his untipped, smokeless Park Drive hung limply from the bottom lip, perhaps in subconscious homage to his irritating but knowledgeable boss.

The atmosphere in the room thickened with the tobacco smoke exhaled by other reporters, leading to the new reporter to wrinkle her snooty nose and give the room a quick squirt of her cologne deodorant. The metallic clamour continued, and Phil produced a torrent of words that were eagerly read by his colleagues before the sheets of paper were dispatched to the sub editors' room on route to the printing press.

In the 1960s a reporter's copy was not highly regarded by other scribes. Stories were scrutinised for faults with spelling or grammar or for gormless typos that would provide material for sneaky jokes over a pint of beer in the pub. That day was different - every word was savoured by his colleagues who knew that something big was breaking- and each sheet of copy was handed from one to another and perused. Several condescended to murmur their approval.

The newcomer, Joan, however, remained aloof from the tumult. Placing her bottle of deodorant back into her leather handbag, she went off to another office to moan to the Editor about the uncivilised behaviour of grammar-school educated journalists and the condition of the smelly office.

In the parlance of the profession, the story took off and soon front pages and TV screens all over the country were filled with the revelation that a body had been found in a secret wartime bunker in Yorkshire.

Journalists from national newspapers and television crews drafted into Northfield were told fanciful stories about the lady in the big house and Bobby Lee. Talkative characters were always rolled out by pranksters in the community when the national media took over the town. Yarns hinting that the infamous duo were having a discrete affair in the black-out were spun, which was palpably untrue, but no-one seemed to mind, particularly readers living in far-off places.

The police soon found themselves in a cul-de-sac. There were no clues in the cellar and nothing new was dug up, so to speak, about the policeman's background. His former wife, now remarried, was traced to her new home on the east coast but did not seem to express any interest in the gruesome discovery. That led one detective to conclude she may have been associated with the death but that turned out to be a fanciful theory as well.

After a few weeks the investigation began to flounder as there were few new leads – the story was therefore relegated from the front to an inside page at the Advertiser – and the journalists employed by the national newspapers returned to their offices in Manchester.

It was left to Ralph, known as the junior, to try to revitalise the story in his naïve way, having overheard Don say he thought black marketeers were responsible for the policeman's demise. There was no evidence to support that argument, but his gut instinct was often correct.

The junior went searching the taprooms to try to find old men who knew what happened in the town during the war. His father had told him stories about the black market and street gangs, though their nefarious activities seemed to have evaded the scrutiny of the local newspaper at the time. Having scoured the yellowing pages of the wartime newspaper files, he had failed to find much material relating to this murky world save for several minor court cases involving small-time racketeers.

At The Albion pub he found Old Bill sitting with a pint of bitter. Oh, yes, the retired miner said, there had been strange goings-on in those dark days and, yes, Miss Elliott and the policeman were involved. How did he know?

"I saw them in the street. Miss Elliott drove off in her Daimler with crates of whiskey in the boot and the bobby stood on the pavement turning a blind eye to the lot. I saw it."

Ralph noticed out of the corner of his eye that the landlord, Dick, was smiling to himself. Even at his tender age the reporter realised Bill may have been trying to con him with the kind of prank which he weaved every time a suited stranger came into the pub to ask questions. Bill distorted what had happened and even made things up, resulting in his pals laughing at his version in the national newspapers or on television. Ralph, in the best tradition of undercover journalists, made an excuse and left but paid for Bill's next pint to show there were no ill feelings.

Chapter 6

The boss was urged to allow him more time to try to find out what had occurred all those years ago but there was other work to do. Time was money according to management who said there were too few reporters to allow a lone wolf to concentrate on an operation that might not result in copy at the end of the week.

"Who is going to fill the paper? "Don remarked one day. "We can't spend too much time on one story. What you want to do just happens in books and films. We'll have to rely on the police to do the leg work then interview their top men in the event of a breakthrough. It's easier than trudging through wet streets and getting threatened. More interesting than burying yourself in piles of old newspapers and reading stories about Bobby chasing ruffians.

"The trouble with this case is that it's so old it's got a beard and anyone who was involved in this wicked act is probably dead along with Bobby. Go back to reporting on council meetings and listening to the dirty bits in the sordid cases we get at court. Just be normal like the rest of our staff.

"Well, not that 'normal'," he grimaced, having

recalled some of the mischievous escapades the youthful ones had got up to in the past. "We do not want you to lose all your innocence at the age of 19. This world is not all about work; at your age you are supposed to have a good time."

With a wicked wink, he gesticulated in the direction of the new reporter sitting with her back to them, hunched over her toy, an ever-reliable Imperial typewriter manufactured in the 1940s.

"Why don't you take her out, get out and about?" Don whispered, his right hand resting on the younger man's left shoulder in a fatherly fashion.

Ralph looked puzzled and whispered back: "Not sure whether I can afford her. The only cocktail bar in town, at the Queen's Hotel, charges a fortune for drinks. That's beyond the aspirations of an impecunious reporter. A pint at the Station Inn costs 1s.6d (6 p) – that's more in my line."

Don looked grave and shook his head. Impecunious – that was a dirty word in the office.

"How many more times, Ralph? Do not use long words. If that was included in one of your articles, the readers would think it was a skin disease."

Sincerity spread across his worn face: "Go on. Just once. Take her out. She may blow you out in bubbles. Holidays laid on in the Caribbean, rides in the back of a Rolls Royce to the Dorchester. In London, mind you, not Northfield."

Joan stopped typing, turned sharply in her chair and gave Don a poisoned look: "What are you two whispering about? I do not have impecunious if that's what you think and unlike your dreadful readers I know what it means. My family is prosperous and far from impecunious.

"If you are talking about my looks and personality, then forget it - I do not fancy him."

Don was downcast. This young woman did not belong to the county class as he believed. Nor was she a sensitive soul.

"I did not mean anything wrong, love," he replied.

"Do not call me love," she fired back. "Why do working class people in this town call each other 'love' even on occasions where romance or love is not involved. Never understood that. 'Love' indeed; you are old enough to be my father."

By now her boss was stuttering, fearful that he would be hauled before the managing director for harassing the blue-eyed girl.

"Everybody says it. I even call Ralph 'love' in my geriatric moments. Doesn't mean anything. It's part of Northfield culture."

She gave Don a piercing look as if questioning his sexuality.

Two days later it was Wednesday morning. The momentum in the office was gathering pace as deadlines approached but there was time for beverages, and it was Ralph's turn to make the coffee and tea. He boiled the kettle in the room they called the kitchen, spooned out instant coffee into ten mugs and added the milk from a bottle that was already past its use by date. For once he remembered to add two lumps of sugar rather than one to Don's morning concoction.

Any gaffe in preparing the drinks always led to a squall of expletives from his colleagues, and particularly Don. Then he carried the drinks on a battered pub tray back to the editorial department.

The office was buzzing, and it had nothing to do with the impending arrival of stomach-churning brews that stoked-up nervous energy for the rest of the day.

Late as usual, Joan had walked in wearing a white almost see-through blouse and the latest daring fashion, a spotlessly white mini skirt. Earlier Susan in reception saw her shapely legs whizzing down the corridor leading from the main entrance and unable to suppress the sensational news about the attire phoned Don in the main office on the first floor. He was told by the excited receptionist that the firm's voluptuous member of the permissive society was hurrying up the staircase to his domain.

Don prepared for the worst, concluding once again that from his experience the pretty ones created most of the trouble in the office. The door swung open and in she rushed, her slipstream making the edges of the pages of newspapers piled deep on a table ripple in apparent awe. The reporters merely gawped at her appearance.

Ralph, carrying his trembling and overloaded tray, was immediately mesmerized by the sight of her sitting languidly in a chair, legs crossed, and chatting to everyone unaware what a sensation she was creating. He walked over to her desk, pausing to hand over a mug of black coffee that was dense enough to keep her awake for weeks. She smiled, said thank you in her silky voice and uncrossed her legs, slowly and provocatively, and he nearly had apoplexy.

The rest of the staff laughed and Ralph, red faced and perspiring, glanced furtively once again at her legs before refocusing onto the calendar on the wall, which displayed a view of a different kind - a pretty photograph of Lake Windermere.

"I thought you were going to ask me out," she whispered once the commotion had died down, the other reporters having turned their attention to the list of engagements assigned to them for the day. "Come on, don't be shy. Just open your mouth."

News about their budding romance circulated through the building and Phil, who was interested in expanding his harem, was jealous and in an act of revenge on his pal revealed an unpleasant truth about his boss's favourite object in the office.

"Well," he told Ralph bluntly. "You can't have the desk tonight. It's off limits."

"Pardon? What desk? What are you talking about?"

"Don's desk of course. Best bit of furniture in the building. Smooth as Beryl's bum and what mahogany. You know what it's used for, don't you? We take our girlfriends into the office in an evening and romp around on the desk. Jolly days.

"Tonight, for instance, I must cover a meeting at the town hall. I shall return with the key to get into the office, type the story and phone a few paragraphs about the meeting to the Yorkshire Post for the morning edition. When all that's done and dusted Beryl and I will start sweating and heaving on his desk."

Ralph was speechless, stammering: "That's disgraceful. That desk is his pride and joy. It's polished to perfection every evening by the cleaners then you lot muck it all up. He would be heartbroken then spiteful if he knew what was happening."

As he walked out of the office, he could not remove the image of that desk and its secret life out of his mind. How long had that kind of thing been going on?

The Edwardian era desk had a worn leather lined top above two frieze drawers and three drawers to each pedestal. It had arrived in the office when the publishers converted the former Victorian town house into its headquarters in the 1920s. Over the decades the premises were refurbished many times and extensions such as a printing works and the managing director's office were built, but the desk was never moved out of the editorial office, remaining virtually in the same spot.

Modern office furniture came and went but not Don's antique gem which turned into a kind of indoor landmark, often catching the studied attention of visitors. It had been kept in an immaculate condition by his predecessors, a series of chief reporters, and was envied by younger members of the present staff who concluded if they could not use it during the day for legitimate reasons then they would purloin it for other purposes in an evening.

Ralph's outrage over the dark secret in the office was heightened by the fact, having worked there for a year, he knew nothing about the sexy goings-on.

Having met Joan in the cocktail bar at the Queens Hotel, he longed for a touch of romance and light relief from concentrating on that dreaded desk.

It was the town's sole AA and RAC rated hotel, a rambling Victorian building which had finally moved into the modern age by the creation of numerous ensuite bedrooms, an almost unknown feature in hotels elsewhere in the town or in other back waters in the north.

The exterior was blackened by decades of smoke and soot, courtesy of countless industrial and domestic fires, and the interior boasted a decent restaurant and an array of welcoming bars that were stated in the Advertiser's advertisements to cater for all tastes. Indeed they did.

He awaited with increasing trepidation the bad news that her cut-glass accent would inevitably announce. What was she going to drink? He glanced at the list on the wall and the prices of the cocktails made him sweat or perspire as she would say.

Half of best bitter in this privileged establishment cost 2s. (25p) – the price of a pint elsewhere - and the barmaid, Betty, disclosed in a posh accent almost as exquisite as Joan's – but not quite - that there was no such thing as a pint of bitter or mild in her shiny emporium.

"If you want a pint you'll have to go into the bottom bar where everything is upholstered and dignified, where there are morning newspapers and the beer is served in pewter tankards and nothing else," added Betty. "That's known as the gentlemen's bar and women are barred. Otherwise, you'll have to go into our lovely lounge where ladies are allowed of course."

She paused for effect, then grimaced.

"Or you can go to Florrie's long bar where the labourers drink. That's where sawdust is used to soak-up messy deposits on the wooden floor. If you want to go there you'll have to use the sole entrance in the back street as there is no internal connecting door save for staff."

Joan shuddered at the thought of meeting the elderly Florrie and her pile of sawdust in the wild saloon. To avoid consternation she smiled and ordered half of Barnsley Bitter, a potent dark brew favoured by miners and steelworkers, after which she held the glass at arm's length and pretended it was champagne. Ralph, relieved, ordered the same but hugged the glass close to his chest on the grounds his hands were trembling in the presence of an attractive woman.

She had managed to surprise him again with her choice of attire that evening, a multicoloured floral short dress which seemed shorter than the one worn on making the grand entrance in the office a few days earlier.

Since that eruption in the office tactics had

changed. To calm the passions of the men and to avert bitchy comments from female colleagues, sedate clothes were worn by her during the day; in cold weather it could well be a brown two-piece made of Donegal-woven tweed, the type of attire her mother may have donned on a Saturday while shopping in Manchester. Flamboyant and sexy clothes were reserved for evenings out.

"Gosh," she asked. "How's the quest going? Have you found Bobby Lee's killer yet?

"No, no," Ralph replied, trying not to look disheartened. "Not had a lot of time. Too many jobs to cover in the evenings, you know. Don keeps me busy because he wants to get my mind off the Lee case. I could crack it in two weeks if I was given plenty of freedom."

"Really?" she replied, not believing him. "Really!"

"Yes," he boasted, now realising his revelation was palpably untrue, but his ego refused to back down and his imagination turned wild.

"Two weeks. That's all it would take and then I would go back to Don's boring tasks.

"I do not like sticking to the assignments handed out by him on the grounds they are second rate. Mundane stuff, really. I like to be a free agent - the loner with a mission. Man against the establishment and all that. That's the kind of news that makes the headlines.

"Do you recall the Hollywood film Call Northside 777? James Stewart was a reporter who campaigned to release a man wrongly accused of murder. That's what it is all about. Justice."

His youthful irreverence coupled with her mild intoxication conspired to change her attitude towards him. She smiled deeply and for the first time in their short working life together there was palpable warmth and sincerity in her face. Her looks were refreshingly youthful, so unlike the other girls in the office who developed a pinched look in their cheeks by their mid -20s. Good looks in either sex never survived long in that brutal but casual office. Ralph, who often contradicted accepted wisdom, blamed the potent coffee.

"How divine," she added, distorting her face, the bitter taste of the beer having lost its initial enchantment. "I'll be able to help. I was stunned on hearing that Mary Elliott had once owned that house of mystery and intrigue. That's good, isn't it? Mystery and intrigue! I am learning the dubious craft of journalism very quickly.

"My father knew Miss Elliott. She loaned him a mountain of money to start a car dealership in the town. I doubt whether she was repaid on the grounds the war and the court case rudely intervened in their business matters. We have some of the old legal documents back home and father still talks about her. He's mentioned a couple of matters that may help you.

"My father said she had a close friend, a farmer who had been an expert in explosives in the first world war and my father did not like him. Thought he was a sinister character. He always said the farm was a front and that his principal income came from stolen goods and the black market. He could have been involved in this mystery, don't you think? Very suspicious. The name is Gerald James. Remember that, darling. It's a secret and do not tell anyone. Between us for the moment.

"There is a drawback to all this. If you hit the jackpot, and I am sure you will, my darling, I want to be involved in the writing of the stories. A couple of long articles of high calibre will be my passport to getting out of this hole and I'll be off to London and beyond, perhaps to America. Right?"

"No problem," he replied, flabbergasted she was taking an interest in him, the youngest in the office and grammar school educated at that. What came next stunned him once again and led to Betty behind the bar looking in amazement at Ralph and in envy at Joan. In shock she stopped rock 'n' rolling the cocktail mixer.

The Advertiser's latest recruit bent forward, revealing ample cleavage and a tantalising promise of possible future amorous activities, and peered firmly into his eyes.

"Ralph," she enquired sultrily. "Do you mind if I ask you something? "

"No, by all means," he replied smiling, hoping he would not be disappointed by her question as he was aware of the way the evening was panning out.

"Do you smoke?"

"Only when I am on fire," he retorted, laughing.

"Okay," she added, licking her lips, "I'll try again.

"I need a cigarette before I go any further. It must be menthol, preferably Swiss."

"Sorry, I cannot help," he replied, becoming tense for a moment as his knowledge of cigarettes was limited to lung-nipping Woodbines and Senior Service.

Then she took a deep breath: "You know, darling, I think I am falling for you. Drat it; I never thought it would happen, particularly with an ex-grammar schoolboy. So many are unsophisticated and uneducated, don't you think? You are different. Good to look at, good to be with. There, I have got it off my chest."

The six-foot reporter with his short coal-black hair and an ear-to-ear smile that suggested Irish ancestry was overjoyed: he walked home with a thrilling new purpose in life.

She's lovely but a little over educated, he concluded.

Chapter 7

Phil, his pal in the office, was working for a spell at a branch office in another town so Ralph went looking for a surrogate mentor on amorous activities. Joan was climbing inside his vulnerable mind without any resistance from him and their friendship was flourishing. He needed advice.

Peter, the well-built Co-op delivery lad, was perfect for the role. Not only a pal he was said to be a Casanova of the streets, having compiled a list of friendly housewives while delivering groceries on the bike around the estates. He chatted them up in the day and returned to their homes in an evening when husbands were on the night shift at the colliery.

A delivery boy may not sound like the type to have the credentials to be the rampant teenage lover of the decade, but he was tall for his age, had dark good looks and cheeky eyes. Fastidious about the appearance of his jet-black hair, he persuaded the barber to add a carefully crafted curl that dangled over the centre of the forehead. It was sometimes known as the Tony Curtis cut after the Hollywood star.

The hair style was called the duck tail in America

and the duck arse in the UK because of the way it swept back and resembled the back end of a duck. Peter, ever the narcissist and proud of his hair, was often caught eyeing himself for long periods in the mirror in the washroom at the back of the Co-op store.

His preoccupation with the appearance of the Hollywood star did not survive long since some girls during that period quickly lost interest in film star lookalikes. The Beatles were taking the world by storm and his hair, in response to popular demand, grew longer and straighter to imitate the Fab Four.

To add to his talents he had an admirable knack of acquiring an arsenal of information from his ladies that made the news columns. According to Don he was better at that task than some of the staff who were paid to do that work. Ralph, who followed up his tip-offs, regarded him as a prized asset for several reasons.

The young newshound rewarded Peter with cups of the new exciting drink, frothy coffee, at a trendy café, The Aloha, where Mods met to talk about girls, Rockers and girls. Phil always arrived there in a smart suit with a neat haircut rather than The Beatles look and riding his Vespa scooter instead of the Co-op. bike.

Peter was found standing astride his bike outside the shop. Of course he wanted to help his pal with tips on love but then pointed to Mrs Bailey's tins of baked beans, jars of jam and packets of Persil in the basket. He seemed to be rather agitated and said he had to be at her house in five minutes.

"Do you get anything apart from money from her?" asked Ralph, grinning, and Peter, winking like a London spiv, rode off without saying anything but Ralph knew the answer.

Ralph could not get his head around technique when it came to the ladies. Chat-up lines devised by his pal were practised in front of the bedroom mirror, but his words always seemed stilted or condescending. As for facial expressions they were ludicrously inane. Peter told him to put passion into efforts to win over a girlfriend but that did not seem to work either and several girls thought he was too forward.

"Oh, Ralph, you are fast," Ann had murmured softly in his ear in the darkness at the cinema. He misinterpreted the soothing words, and she soon wriggled out of his arms to move away from his fidgety fingers. "Get off!!"

Most of his girls were like Back Row Annie – "An iceberg," he told Peter, who later bemoaned his lack of charisma. But Joan was a revelation. Nothing had happened on their first date - despite the highly suggestive conversation - but he was determined to try harder next time. He had to grow-up sometime, his pals were told.

The following morning the new love of his life, Joan, was forgotten for a few hours because Don said the Editor wanted to see him.

"He's getting worried about you," confided Don, genuinely concerned for his welfare as the youngster seemed to be skipping meals and failing to maintain his usual smart appearance.

In his office Ron asked him to sit down, handing over one of his Senior Service cigarettes. It was a routine gesture on his part since he thought that men who did not smoke were effeminate. Those who refused were given a black look and basically put out to grass.

Ralph did not smoke much but knew all about the theory and so lit up and sat back with a deeply self -satisfied expression, as detectives did on solving a murder in the final scene of old black-and-white films.

"Right, young man," said Ron. "You have been working too hard, Ralph, and it's time you gave up on the Lee case. It's going to go on forever and they'll be investigating who did it in another 20 years. Mark my words.

"Miss Elliott did not have a key to that bunker, so she's out of the equation. No-one apart from the policeman and several local VIPs, plus the men who would be housed there of course, knew of its existence. Not even the policeman's superiors. It was on the top-secret list. We'll never know why Lee walked to the house and why he was lured into the tunnels and killed. You have found yourself entangled in a nightmare. It's not worth it.

"You have got to hand it to old Mary. She conned the town and the government into thinking she was respectable. Whitehall and military commanders took one look at her house and her character and put the bunker underground at Two Trees. Perfect, they said, and the top brass were hoodwinked. It's a pity she was not in charge of British intelligence during the war – she could have used her talents to deceive the Germans.

"Anyway, find yourself a steady girlfriend and enjoy yourself. They say Joan is interested. Why not take her out again and walk on the wild side for a change?"

So that's what they did. In her Austin Healey Sprite sports car the two juniors were soon speeding along winding country roads, following up stories together and popping into a pub for a drink and a meal at lunchtime. It was the freedom they enjoyed most, that elusive escape route from the dreary office that was much sought after by the staff – even the Editor couldn't wait to attend Rotary Club lunches at the Queen's Hotel on a Tuesday lunchtime.

Their personalities gelled. She descended from her haughty tower in a graceful fashion and Ralph was hooked for life. And life meant life to him.

On sunny afternoons at weekends they walked through woodland or down lanes, enjoying each other's company and planning long weekends away together. Back in the office no-one seemed to mind that they spent so much time together while working, provided they turned in the stories for publication on time, and someone pointed out that they were always smiling and at ease with each other.

One day while walking hand in hand along the High Street Peter pedalled by on his bike, giving them an exaggerated thumbs up sign. The jaunty delivery boy, who thought their romance was down to his sound advice, was thankful he could promote heavenly relationships as well as break marital homes.

At the hotel one evening Ralph asked his new love: "Why did you come to work at the Advertiser? You could have worked on a provincial evening or morning newspaper in a city and earned more money."

"It's my father," she replied, gloomily.

"Self-made man. The family can't contradict him. He believes everyone should have a spell working at the bottom of the career ladder. Get to know the ropes without too much pressure. He knows your Editor and believes I could learn the basics before moving south."

Despite the harmony the couple could not have been more different, a case of opposites attracting, according to pals.

Ambitious Joan decided to be a journalist having witnessed a mountain rescue in the Alps while on a school field trip. The following day she read an account of the operation in the International Herald Tribune, the American owned newspaper published in Paris and widely read in cultured circles in western Europe. That set her off on her career path with help from her father.

Unambitious Ralph also had help from his father on his journey through life. He was taken down the mine on a Sunday as a 14-year-old. Top management were absent on that day and his father's colleague, a deputy, turned a blind eye to what was happening since it was illegal to take someone so young underground without authorisation. In a dusty and hot seam he saw and heard men swearing, sweating and working hard: "This is going to happen to you unless you pass your examinations," father warned.

As a result, newspapers preoccupied his spare time. Not the International Herald Tribune which he had never heard of but the lowly Advertiser and the Sheffield Star, the regional evening. Having gained three GCE 'O' levels he went to work at the weekly newspaper.

There were other differences. She handled her open topped expensive car with panache; he travelled to work on a double-deck bus and went on jobs in the old Morris driven by a short-sighted photographer.

She was ex-finishing school, her father was loaded, and the family lived in a large house in the VIP end of town; Ralph left school aged 17 and resided with his parents in a terraced house with an outside lavatory.

She bought short skirts and dresses with bold designs in person from Mary Quant's first boutique, Bazaar, in Chelsea. He relied on ready-to-wear suits for work from Burtons, one of the multiple tailors, and occasionally bought a much-prized made-to-measure creation – minus unfashionable lapels - with drainpipe trousers from a bespoke tailor in Northfield.

The chasm between backgrounds led to friends poking fun but the entertainment ceased once the relationship became serious. That's when their families started to worry, the parents believing each had selected a companion from the wrong class.

The sedate cocktail bar at the Queens Hotel, with its shady lamps, trendy white half-moon bar and reclining leather chairs, became their second home where they imbibed on equal terms. She drew the red line at what she thought was a rough pub, The Gardeners, his local, and she persevered with the draught beer at the hotel on the grounds she respected his northern meanness. Or so she said. Ralph, however, always missed her sour expression when venturing to take a third sip of the evening.

Chapter 8

Joan was born in Northfield but had spent little time there due to her education at private schools. Her knowledge of the locality and its inhabitants, particularly the working class, the backbone of the newspaper's readership, was non-existent. In the course of the new job she was meeting people whom she thought were strange and out of step with the 20th century.

On an assignment with Phil she was shocked when they drove up to a terraced house in one of the close-knit settlements built near one of the mines 100 years earlier.

The door was opened by a grey-haired woman who looked much older than her years. They were told to return when the 'Mester' was in as she was not permitted at home to talk to strangers on her own.

While outlining the story one evening in the bar, she gave Ralph a puzzled look: "What's a Mester? Why wouldn't she let us in. It was only a golden wedding anniversary article after all. A few innocuous questions and answers and then the ordeal for them was over."

His reply: "That's not unusual at all. 'Mester'

means the man, the boss of the house. A lot of these people were brought up in the 1920s and their lives have not changed except there is a TV in the living room. The man appears to oversee the household but isn't really the boss and women rule the roost."

She smiled: "It was quite funny. We went back in the afternoon and Mester was in. He sat at the kitchen table reading the morning newspaper, which was propped up by a bottle of HP sauce and a dirty milk bottle. Never said a word. She, however, rabbited on about their life together and we couldn't stop her. There are peculiar people in Northfield."

He wondered what she would think about her first visit to his terraced home, much superior to 'Mester's' abode but much inferior to her family's house. The look on his father's face when she drew up in her flash car remained with him for years. His parents gazed out from behind the lace curtains as he climbed into the passenger seat and on returning from a trip to the Peak District was given a short lecture on declining moral standards in the permissive 1960s. Obviously, his father – like many miners a non-drinker and a puritan - did not approve of the mini skirt.

"She's probably a very nice girl but not for our Ralph," he told his wife, who did not say but thought that all men were out for what they could get – including dear Ralph. Her mother thought the same about her liberated daughter who was obviously infatuated, but men of inferior status were always expendable in their ruthless world that thrived in the snobbish end of town.

The Editor had recommended a walk on the wild side. That occurred one evening when she had too much to drink at the hotel and the allure of a bed triumphed while her parents were away on holiday abroad. Peter the delivery boy's sure-fire advice on how to woo a lady came to mind while lovemaking, but that night he did not take much notice since everything seemed to come naturally, and she responded with a vitality and an intimate knowledge of his sensitive physical spots that came as a surprise.

The next morning Joan, snuggling naked under a sheet on the bed, giggled and said: "We are supposed to be finding Bobby Lee's killer and by now I should be writing the story, not just for the Advertiser but for The Daily Mail and The LA Times as well.

"Readers ought to be devouring details about the life of the missing policeman, the man who had the looks of one of those Hollywood idols in the 1940s and who had a string of female fans and lovers. Instead, I have spent too much time typing results from the garden and chrysanthemum society, the canine society, the swimming galas, school sports days and village galas.

"Egg and spoon race: 1,2,3, Adolf Hitler. Himmler was a poor 5th in that contest. That's what I wanted to write the other afternoon in the office while peering at the sports day results scribbled on paper by an illiterate teacher. Obedient as per usual I used the real names at the last moment to avert a rollicking from Don. Does anyone read that kind of thing? Who cares save his mum, Mrs Hitler?"

"Not really but at least it improves a trainee's mental discipline," came the pompous reply. "Spent my early days typing that stuff from the garden society shows. Chrysanthemums: incurved: 1, Smith; 2, Clarke; 3 P Quinn. If you can concentrate on that material and complete the lot without a mistake or losing your temper then you can concentrate on anything, even the mayor's verbose speeches. That's what Don calls sound training. It's more important than digesting the law of libel in a stuffy book. We have not been sued for years because Don makes sure of that. He has an acute eye for defamation of character and is known in the trade as a good operator."

"Balderdash," she said, spitefully. "What's all this nonsense, darling? Don says this and Don says that. The last time he did anything was at the Battle of Balaclava. I'm not sure what Freud would make of you. Perhaps your parents have landed you with a father complex. You fawn over him."

Then his grin broadened. "Your 1,2,3, A. Hitler reminds me of the day when a junior reporter on a Lancashire weekly newspaper managed to include all the names of the Manchester United football team in a list of mourners at a retired clerk's funeral. The sub editor checking the report was a woman who knew bugger all about football.

"On reading the newspaper to check whether Auntie Dot and Uncle Bill's names were included in the list of mourners, the deceased's daughter could not understand what Bobby Charlton was doing at the funeral and why she had not recognised him. Then the Third World War broke out and the reporter got the boot. He had been bored stiff, having spent too much time typing the names of mourners in obits and had his little nervous breakdown. Happy times."

She feigned glumness and thought of the elderly mayor of Northfield and his verbose speeches. He was enjoying his final splurge of civic duties and freebies before the political party pitch-forked him into retirement.

"I had forgotten about that gold nugget of a job. It must be spiffing to watch that geriatric dribbling moist words onto the heads of the school choir sitting near the podium at the annual speech day. I do not usually say 'spiffing' but it does upset your working-class sensibilities and I enjoy doing that. Smile, Ralph, I didn't mean it."

There was one last experience at work that puzzled her.

"You know, I went to see this guy," she said. "He got nasty for no apparent reason. At the end of the rant against reporters he asked how much the newspaper cost and how many copies were sold per week.

"I told him 3 pence and 40,000 copies. Then he said that this week the figure would be 39,999 because he was going to cancel his regular order. What was all that about? I never said a wrong word to him."

Ralph replied: "He probably had something

against the newspaper and wanted to get his own back by having a go at a member of staff. Make them feel small for his own irrational gratification. I doubt whether he bought the paper. A genuine nut case."

Thanks to her lover she was finally beginning to understand Northfield, its off-beat occupants and that other enigma, the world of newspapers and their readers.

Chapter 9

Soon their dull evenings composed of leisurely discussions about flower shows and the ramblings of the almost senile mayor were over: the cold case came out of the past. Little Jimmy, who had supplied the village policeman with a plethora of jokes all those years ago, was now a man mountain with two children. One day he walked into reception at the Advertiser and asked for Ralph.

"Is there anywhere we can go, private-like?" he asked. "It's about P.c. Lee and Mary Elliott. Something has come up and I'm still recovering from the shock. I'm on my way to the police station but I thought I would drop off here first since I know from your stories in the newspaper that you are interested in what happened."

After settling down in the interview room adjacent to reception, Jimmy poured out his story. Two days earlier while renovating his parents' former home a large cardboard box had been found at the bottom of a wardrobe.

"This is what I came across," he added, producing from a shopping bag a collection of letters and an Enfield .45 army service revolver.

"Good grief," said Ralph, taken back. "What's all this? Is that gun real?"

"It's real all right." Jimmy replied. "There is ammunition back home. I never realised that my father, who had been in the army during the first world war, was one of the locals picked to man that bunker at Miss Elliott's house. He never breathed a word about that place. But there is new information in some old letters I have found. Both my father and the policeman knew each other and met underground to talk about what would happen if the enemy paratroopers landed.

"Rumours about invading Germans went round the village in those days. My mother got upset one day when one of the neighbours said paratroopers had landed in Doncaster, 12 miles away, and that it was true as the neighbour's brother worked at the town hall and had heard it for a fact. Just daft talk but scare stories were prevalent at the time."

Jimmy was known as 'smiler' at the colliery because of his permanent grin. Not on that afternoon at the Advertiser office, he was downcast, pointing out that his father's skills as a poacher were seen as useful had the bunker been taken over by the guerilla squad. Too many secrets were tumbling out of the family archives, and he couldn't cope.

There was more to come. According to the letters written between his father and a brother living in the south, his father knew all the locals who were actively involved in the black market, who drove the lorries carrying the illegal goods and who made money out of the racket. The gang even used the bunker as its headquarters, an outrageous clandestine manoeuvre that the top brass failed to detect, for Churchill's Secret Army was too secret for its own good.

"There are ten names on a list he compiled and several of those men are still around. According to my mother the list and other details were kept in the safe at a solicitor's office in Northfield after the war, with an accompanying message saying it had to be handed over to the police in the event of anything happening to him.

"The solicitor's office closed a couple of years ago, the list was returned, and my father kept it in the box in the wardrobe. My mother died four years' ago and father six months' ago."

The latest revelations numbed Ralph's inquisitive mind for several seconds before he conducted a thorough interview. A photographer was called to take a picture of the weapon for that week's edition. Was it the one used to kill Bobby?

"Then there is this card," added Jimmy. "At first glance it looks a business card but what do the words 'Catch Me If You Can' mean? That's all that's on the card. No name."

Ralph: "Very strange, no idea what it is."

At the cocktail bar in the evening Ralph and Joan exchanged views and prepared a strategy for the future. She said: "What I did not understand about this affair in the early days was that you were beaten up and you thought it was something to do with the case. I couldn't see that. I thought it was just a thug wanting some jolly entertainment on a Friday night in Northfield.

"Today's interview has changed all that. If there are guilty men on Jimmy's list, then perhaps there are people out there who are prepared to kill or break a few bones to ensure the mystery is never solved.

"What do we do now? I want to get some action, so I am not seconded on to what I have termed the stupid news unit in the office, i.e. the one where you are expected to type the results of some bizarre gala. There's the Yorkshire miners' jamboree coming up in Northfield. There'll be 100,000 people there and trying to wrestle with all those results of the Coal Queen and bonny baby competitions, plus flower and pet shows, will shred my nerves. On top of that the political speeches demonising the poor old Tories will put me in a mental institution."

With £1 and 10s notes (50p) poised to flee his wallet, Ralph was living the high life with his girl on pay day, treating himself to an expensive martini, 'shaken but not stirred' as in a James Bond film.

Betty was told to give the shiny metal container the 'hippy hippy shake' to make a couple of decent drinks and she responded with an awesome burst of energy, shaking and juggling the mixer, and thereby providing impromptu entertainment for the well-heeled set standing at the other end of the bar.

The secret agent on the big screen took time off from the tedious business of espionage to focus on the ladies and the equally suave Ralph, on Friday evenings at any rate, did the same. He enjoyed forgetting about the office and instead put his feet up, on this occasion concentrating on his girlfriend's lovely legs and her skirt which, unbelievably, seemed to be shorter than her others. That's impossible, he thought.

"Joan, your skirt? It's even shorter than before. It's getting embarrassing. That guy sitting over there has never taken his eyes off you. Or parts of you."

She was annoyed. "We are not supposed to be talking about my legs, darling. Why have you become such a prude? What's that working-class term? Is it 'pr**k'? Are you taking after your father? What are you going to say when I wear a topless dress? That's going to be the next big trend."

He was poised to say she wouldn't dare but kept quiet on the grounds she concealed a variety of eye-watering facial slaps which, like wartime German Stuka dive bombers, came out of the blue.

"Take a sedative, Ralph. Let's concentrate on work, shall we?" she asserted. "What are we going to do about our sizzling little story? Do not worry, Bobby Lee, we'll find your killer."

Placing the cocktail on the table, he said: "I'll have a word with the police and find out what they want to disclose and perhaps, just perhaps, get a look at the names on that list. Jimmy refused to show it to me, but a friendly copper may do us a favour. I may have to trade in something for such a belter of a disclosure. Perhaps Don would allow us to give the police a load of publicity regarding their latest drink driving campaign.

"That's boring material to us and the readers but that kind of thing works with the police who are very much into improving public relations. There's talk of the police using something called breathalysers to clamp down on motorists' drinking, so they may send out a press release on that subject. Breathalysers? Seems a daft idea to me. As my mother says, what will they think of next?"

The alcohol in the potent martini momentarily paralysed the rational side of his mind and her face-slapping dive-bombers were forgotten. He committed a cardinal blunder by antagonising her.

"As for you, Joan, why don't you wear longer skirts or dresses? Phil is always hanging around you in the office like a starving dog and that's what he is when it comes to women, a dog. You are not much better if you like him. Why not tell him to get lost?"

"Not likely," she retorted angrily, giving him one of her black looks. "I hope that was a bad joke?"

"Yes."

His mind was numbed once more, not by alcohol but by a furious blow, the sound of which was heard in the neighbouring Florrie's bar where the merry Irish contingent downed pints on an industrial scale. Like the crack of a sniper's rifle during the 1916 Rebellion in Dublin, one declared with a self-satisfied grin.

She also had the last punitive word: "That martini does not suit you, Ralph. You are not quite sophisticated enough, you are devoid of polish, more a bit of rough. Perhaps a pint of bitter and a Woodbine cigarette with dangling ash are more in your line. You are a Don cardboard cut-out. Downbeat and obtuse."

He became serious: "Something is happening to our relationship. A spot of aggro is creeping in, and I am as bad as you. I wonder whether we are spending too much time together and getting on each other's nerves."

She remained silent for a moment and then smiled. Her ability to recover from a bout of typhoon-like fury never failed to amaze him.

"My mental explosions are disturbing, according to my father," she admitted. "They do not last, however, and I am soon back to my normal self. You do not realise our relationship is based on tension, conflict and love, with the emphasis on the latter.

"My lone grumble with you is that you never say 'I love you' unless I drag it out of you. You are afraid to show your emotions. I am always saying 'I love you' but you just clam up. Yet I know how you feel. You do not realise a lady still likes to hear nice words, makes her feel better, more conducive to your charms.

"Lighten-up. Take a few tips from Peter the bicycle man. Meanwhile, I'll treat you. Time you had a touch of culture, getaway from Northfield and its horrors. We'll go to the Royal Albert Hall in London, then to my favourite Hungarian restaurant and afterwards I'll give you a decent rogering at The Hilton. It will be a real thrill, and it will be my pleasure."

"That's an interesting proposition," he replied

coolly, glancing at the barmaid to try to gauge her reaction to such a startling suggestion before returning his undivided attention to Joan.

Betty, drying a martini glass, remained stony-faced and silent but continued to be emotionally interested in the long-term impact of the skirmish between the couple.

Chapter 10

The interview with Jimmy was written up by them for that week's edition, the silly rumpus in the hotel having been forgotten. Their skills and thoughts fused, and Don smiled in admiration. He had never seen such close co-operation between two reporters for years.

"It was as though electricity was sparking from the metal keys of the typewriter," he told his wife in one of his purple prose moods while watching television in the evening. "They are so close. They operate as one. Not seen anything like that for years. Poetry. But I have that funny feeling it won't last. It's too good to be true."

The duo went into detail, referring to clandestine meetings in the bunker between the gang and the policeman in the 1940s, outlining the activities of the black marketeers and mentioning the service gun. However, they did not speculate when it came to names for legal reasons.

Quotes from the police added authenticity to any startling narrative. The Editor knew that some readers would not believe what they read without the inclusion of the local inspector's name in the story. It was the kind of news that went beyond what the public expected from the local newspaper and the police chief's anodyne remarks were inserted immediately before what was known as 'ends', the term typed by all reporters to denote 'the end' of an article. He confirmed a police investigation was under way but did not go into details.

The following week she went off to interview Jimmy again in case there had been new developments. It transpired that because of the previous story some neighbours were not talking to him, and he had received several sinister phone calls: the caller remained silent at the end of the line for about 15 seconds then put down the receiver. By calling in the newspaper he had broken the village's dubious code of honour.

On returning to the office, having felt that someone was stalking her near Jimmy's home, she told Don and Ralph that the case was becoming weird. She believed there was something deeper going on below the surface, something mysterious and that the probing into what could be the heart of the criminal world was beginning to unsettle her. Ralph, ever the hero to help a lady in distress, promised to cover the aspects of the case she did not like.

That evening the couple cuddled up together in bed, having obtained through her long list of wealthy acquaintances the part-time use of a flat just outside Northfield. It was a cosy refuge where they pursued their own way of life at weekends without interference from parents or the office.

He was stroking her long black hair and kissing her gently on the neck while she slept. He was so lucky. Six months earlier his shyness with the opposite sex had convinced him the acquisition of any girlfriend was beyond him. Now there was Joan who was both attractive and intelligent. He was so glad they were getting closer and that their emotions were maturing in unison.

She was more anxious. The fall-out from the Bobby Lee case had rattled her and every time an oak tree branch scraped the bedroom window in the wind in the early hours, she awoke and flinched, believing for a few seconds there was something witchy in the darkness.

"What's that?" she asked anxiously. "That noise."

"Just the wind," he answered, then he pushed the button marked how-to-make-a-girl nervous.

"Perhaps a rat."

She shuddered: something ugly from the future had crept into the bedroom. Then she looked sheepish, for she did not want to exhibit any kind of weakness in his presence and turned over and went back to sleep.

What she did not know was that he was so helplessly in love that any eruption in the relationship would send him spiralling into a crisis that would threaten the foundations on which his personality was based. All that was a long way off.

The following day the two reporters spent the

office hours doing routine work – though Joan managed to avoid the dreadful gala results which were typed up by the Editor's secretary – and as the clock reached 5pm, the end of the working day, Don asked how the Lee affair was going. He was still keen to know what had happened all those years ago.

"Not a lot, Don, I am afraid," replied Ralph. "The police do not seem to have done all that much and they wouldn't allow me to have a glance at their list of suspects while they looked the other way. I think those halcyon moments between police and journalists have gone; there is no chumminess between us these days."

"Really?" replied Don, smiling to himself. "I'll see what I can do."

That's a joke, Joan thought. How could a man who was obviously past it do anything? He spent most of his time smoking and living in the past, but she kept her mouth shut until returning home.

That evening the phone rang. The man at the end of the line coughed and Ralph knew it was Woody Woodbine, Don's new nickname.

"I have had a word with someone, one of my old police contacts. Don't say anything at all about my involvement, not even to the Editor. There are three survivors on that list, Brian Burrows, Phil Casey and Gerald James, that farmer, a sinister character according to Joan. The rest of the gang are in the cemetery. You'll have to speed-up, or someone will be arrested before you have time to put a slip of paper in the typewriter. Once someone is arrested there is little we can do until the court case. Goodnight."

Don never failed to surprise him. Half the time in the office he appeared to be sleep-walking through to retirement but when the chips were down, he pulled something out of the hat, Ralph concluded to himself. He then berated himself in a humorous way, having resorted to cliches with 'chips were down' and 'pulled something out of the hat.'

The use of cliches was akin to a crime in Don's opinion and young reporters received a scolding in front of the office when using such distasteful phrases in copy. The biggest surprise was that Don, born in a terraced house, appeared to have something in common with Joan's elite tutors in Lucerne who also felt that cliches were repellent.

"Who was on the phone, darling?" Joan asked.

"No-one really, just a call from a contact at the parish church."

That was the first and last time he lied to her. He didn't want her to be involved in tracking the three suspects since she was becoming too nervous and there was going to be trouble.

Brian Burrows was first on the list. His name did not appear to be in the telephone directory, but his address was found in the electors' list at the library. As usual Peter the Co-op delivery youth's comprehensive local knowledge came in useful and soon Ralph had built-up a biography of the man. He was a retired miner and petty criminal whose name appeared on numerous magistrates' case lists which Don scrutinised every week to assess whether they were worth covering by reporters.

"What do you want?" Burrows, a squat man with a fiercely red face, bald head and large nervous eyes, was standing on the doorstep. He also had the largest hands Ralph had ever seen, knuckled-hard and hairy, and he may have met their acquaintance before, perhaps in a dark alleyway on a Saturday several months earlier. Street fighting was not unknown to teenage lads in Northfield.

"The police have already been here, and they have nothing on me. You are barking up the wrong tree as usual. I wouldn't help you anyway. I never liked my name being plastered over your rag when I was in trouble with the police."

Ralph interviewed a couple of neighbours, but his best information came from Mark Pinder, the ex-miner and union branch official whose son was destined to become the local MP.

"Brian Burrows worked with me down the pit for years," Mark, senior, said. "Not the brightest button and a petty criminal as well. Despite what has been said he was not associated with the black market, and he is not a killer despite the size of his fists. He doesn't have the streak in him. Someone must have been playing silly buggers when his name was mentioned. Now that farmer called Gerald James is another matter. Devious as they come."

Having given Ralph what he wanted, Mark asked a favour, a normal procedure in the tit-for-tat world of journalism.

"My son Mark is destined to climb the political

ladder. The union will help him get elected as a Labour councillor. While still young, he'll be in line to be the MP since in this town almost everyone votes for that party. He'll need a good contact on the local newspaper, and you are just the man. You are both on the same wavelength and understand each other. Once elected as MP he'll slip you good stories and he'll expect good coverage. Okay?"

The next man on the notorious list proved to be a non-starter as well and Ralph was beginning to believe Don had selected the names at random to try to impress his colleagues he was still well informed on his patch. Like any good journalist, Ralph asked an experienced reporter to check with an unofficial source at the police station and the names of the suspects on the list turned out to be correct. Don, as usual, was right.

But why was the newspaper investigation faltering? Had the man who had compiled the list all those years ago included the names of innocent men on the list for some arcane reason?

Chapter 11

While juggling routine work with his growing obsession with the Lee case, Ralph was summoned to reception where a white-haired lady resembling his vision of a retired spinster schoolteacher was waiting.

"You do not know who I am, do you?" she asked, giggling like a girl. Oh dear, he thought, another dud interview, another waste of time. An old woman with dreary memories of life in Northfield in the 1920s. How wrong he was.

With eyes twinkling, she tantalised him by tittering: "Had you been around in the old days you would have known. Come on you can't be that obtuse. Everyone knew me in Gorton. Lady Bountiful?"

"Miss Elliott," he replied, astonished, and perhaps overawed at meeting someone with such a notorious reputation. "Where have you come from? I can't believe it."

She asked politely: "Is there somewhere we can go that's private?"

His visitor was small, plump and looked older than her years. Her hair was lifeless, she had heavy bags under her eyes and a double chin that wobbled when she became excited. Her tweedy two piece and wide brimmed hat were neat but redolent of the 1930s and mothballs. But there was something endearing about her dottiness and pleasant nature, like the appeal of a favourite elderly aunt.

"I have done my time as they say in the American movies," she said, unashamedly. "Taken the rap."

The American phrase took him by surprise as it wasn't the kind of thing such a well-educated woman was supposed to utter. She was beginning to fascinate him. A one off, he thought, and full of surprises - like a silver-haired version of Joan.

How could this little lady who kept morale upbeat during the war by giving patriotic talks in an evening at the local welfare hall blow thousands of £s on extravagant living.

Then he remembered that an old uncle once told his father that the number of small businesses mushroomed in Northfield during her free spending years, and that she sometimes never asked to be repaid.

She continued: "I've been a free for years and live elsewhere in genteel poverty. I have good friends who send copies of the Advertiser. One of my friends has brought me over here in their car.

"You have been busy, haven't you? You are getting close to something that may blow the top off this town. I do not know a lot, you know, but I can help. The government said at the start of the war the bunker was going to be built under my home and gardens and that was it. The engineers and tunnellers moved in and I went along with it.

"I had romantic visions of entertaining our dashing army officers in my home when I heard it could become part of a regiment's headquarters, if things became messy. Then, as the war reached a critical phase in the early years, I thought the wretched German SS would shortly supplant them since they could have taken a liking to the house as well.

"Before the war I was a Nazi sympathiser for a year, having enjoyed a motoring holiday over there, and the Germans were so warm and generous. However, when hostilities broke out I became an ardent patriot again. Fancy the thought of all those Nazis drinking fine wine in my home, with our lads hiding underground and preparing to pounce and give the beasts a good hiding. Unfortunately, I have always had a vivid imagination. Of course, you are too young to remember those days.

"P.c Lee had a key to my front door and would sometimes go across the reception area and down the steps into the cellar, but I rarely saw him. When he disappeared, someone said he had gone off with another woman and I believed the story. Also, I did not want the police hanging around my place for obvious reasons. A policeman in the search party found what you called the secret door, but his superiors were scared off by the secret service and the underground rooms were never examined. Not that they would have found anything since Bobby by then was a few feet under the wooden floor.

"I never realized until the newspaper's recent disclosure that the policeman's body was down there. Never in this world. The police interviewed me when the skeleton was found but they soon realised I was not involved all those years ago. It's not in my nature. Spending other people's money on a grand lifestyle is but not killing, which is a messy business.

"Which leads me to tell you something that you don't know. I always liked what the Advertiser said about me in the old days before the roof fell in. 'An esteemed figure in the community' were the operative words that come to mind.

"Well," she added, her eyes sparking with mischief. "Bobby Lee wasn't the only person entombed there. You didn't know that did you? Nor do the police; I never said a word when they came to see me the other week. One of the black marketeers is there, too. Somewhere, not sure where.

"A local member of the squad destined to be based there during emergencies was never properly screened by the security services or our local VIPs. He had no criminal record but was crooked all the same. Took advantage of this secret place and stored black-market goods down there. The crooks always entered through the escape exit in the garden. I never said anything because I did not want the police popping round. One day a man who double-crossed the leader was... what do the Americans call it? Bumped off - that's it. Gangster-speak."

To Ralph's annoyance her mind wandered: "I loved gangster talk in the movies, you know. On an evening I would creep out of Two Trees and head for the local cinema. Loved crime films with James Cagney. However, my favourite star was William Holden.."

Agitated, Ralph interrupted her flow: "Yes, yes, Miss Elliott. Very interesting indeed but what happened after he was…err. Bumped off?"

"Oh, yes, where was I? Bumped off. Rubbed out. Same thing. Yes. I was standing at the top of the cellar steps when the second killing took place. The so-called secret door was open, I heard conversations and the sound of the gun. It was not difficult to put two and two together and I went off on holiday for several weeks to keep out of the way. I had enough trouble as it was without getting involved in their wicked deeds."

Ralph had never heard anything like it before. Was she hallucinating? Or mad?

She went on: "My shrinks thought I lived in an Alice in Wonderland world, but I like to think I brought a touch of the rapaciousness enjoyed by pirates to my otherwise conventional persona. In other words I became tired of being nice and proper. I wanted to kick over the traces and kick the pit owners as well. I hoisted the Jolly Roger, you could say.

He hesitated for a moment before asking: "Really? Surely not. There must have been other reasons than just being a rebel. The company had looked after you all your working life."

Replying, she said: "I went to private school. All

my friends had loads of money, and their parents channelled a lot of it into charities. I wanted to do the same, but I didn't have the money, so I clipped the foliage from the company's money tree. I also believed I was underpaid by mean directors.

"I paid for all the uniforms for the scouts and girl guides. They came round to the house to be fitted out. I loved the joy on the faces of those youngsters.

"My miniature railway in the grounds was very popular with the children, you know. Old Bill Hardy was the engine driver. He drove the train as though it was The Flying Scotsman. On one occasion it nearly came off the rails and the children did not seem to mind. We had garden parties there and families rolled up in droves. Happy days. Lots of money was raised for charity.

"A good time was had by all. Do you hacks still use such a term? I always believed it was a cliché, not the sort of word to be produced by a decent brain."

Ralph frowned: "Please do not start... sounds like my boss, Don. He's always on about them. Treats cliches like vermin."

Surprised she replied: "Pardon... really?"

"Never mind, carry on, Miss Elliott."

She continued: "All those suited men in our office at the mine never suspected a thing. They never realised I was taking money out of the company. All the best brains were in the Army or RAF and all the pretty secretaries must have distracted the incumbents. There was only one person who realised what was happening, a grizzled old miner who went to the dinners held for the elderly at Christmas.

"After I had delivered a welcoming speech one year, he came over, found a quiet corner and said: 'I know what you are up to, Mary, but I do not mind. You are diddling the directors out of their money, and I like that. You are taking the rich for a ride. About time. Do not worry, I won't say anything; I enjoy my dinners at Christmas too much'.

"Did it all with a nod and a wink. I do not know how he knew what was going on. Perhaps he was a good judge of character. Never saw him again. I often wonder what happened to him."

That was it. Having unloaded her guilt, she felt happy. She said goodbye, wishing Ralph all the best in his efforts to discover the truth about the mystery hidden away at Two Trees.

"Well, I am off. I am going to walk down Market Hill and visit a couple of stores. It's time to do some shoplifting. Surprised? You shouldn't be. Now don't go phoning the shopkeepers or the police. Do me one last favour. Then I am off to look at Two Trees. They tell me it's gone downhill since I left.

"I never finish talking, you know. I say I am leaving company then change my mind as there is always something else to say. A word of warning, young man. There is a family around here called Pinder. Have you heard of them? Perhaps not, they are a secret lot and no good. They were involved in the black market during the war.

"I may as well tell you the important bit. The villain you are seeking is a member of that family –

but you'll have to find his first name. I am not going too far; I do not like making it too easy for anyone.

"People will say I do not like the Pinders because another member, a union leader, criticised my short-term loyalty to Adolf Hitler. That's not true. They are no good, that's it. A case of the kettle calling the frying pan black. Perhaps. Take care. Be careful I do not return to play tricks on you... after I am dead of course."

"What about Gerald James, the farmer who lived near Two Trees?" asked Ralph, worried she would leave the office without disclosing more important information.

"No, no nothing wrong with him," she replied, giving Ralph a peculiar look. "People did not like him. Looked like Raymond Massey who played villains in Hollywood films. I think his looks put the locals off him. People made up stories about the poor man. Had he resembled William Holden there would not have been a problem. That's why the villagers liked Bobby Lee. He looked like the golden boy Holden."

Smiling wryly, he shook his head as she walked out of the office with the aid of her walking stick. It never occurred to him to tip-off the staff in the shops, not after getting such an exclusive. As for the Pinder family? That couldn't be true –he liked them.

That evening in the hotel, Ralph was in a reflective mood.

"You know, Joan, I cannot get over it. Miss Elliott. After all the years and all the articles I have finally met her. I have read all the transcripts of the court case and Don has told us lots of stories saying she was evil and a criminal, but I still can't believe it. She was just a nice old lady. Potty, perhaps, but that was it. Some people do lead double lives. I wonder what will happen to her?"

"Die," a bored Joan said. "Happens all the time."

The following day, having listened to the latest disclosures by Mary, Don thought Ralph was the delusional one as the story seemed to be beyond belief.

"Are you on drugs?" he asked. "Your generation seems to be hooked on them. All this flower power and summers of love we get these days. Don't know what the world is coming to, I really don't."

Every couple of minutes he changed his attitude, his mind racing from one theory to another and for the first time in years he was out of his comfort zone while discussing a tricky story.

"Are you sure she was Miss Elliott? It could have been someone else down the street who wants to hoodwink the Advertiser. Have a laugh at our expense. No; that can't be right on second thoughts. Ralph you must be the one at fault. This story is too fantastic. Do you think you should have a check-up? On the other hand, if the story is true who is the gang leader and is he alive?

Ralph was more composed: "We can't print anything. It's all circumstantial and we can't depend on Miss Elliott as she is not a copper-bottomed witness. She's probably still nuts and if she's wrong we'll look daft. There is another reason why I do not want to contact the police. Why make life easier for them? We could keep quiet and try to find the leader on our own."

Don: "Find Phil and grab your girlfriend on the way. No, Ralph, not in that fashion; you have no need to grin. Go for it. No, no, that's not right either. Too rude.

"Make some enquiries but don't spend too long on this case, otherwise we'll never produce a newspaper on time. There are plenty of other stories that need your attention."

Ralph and Phil teamed up at Florrie's bar, where life was more relaxed and much cheaper than elsewhere in the hotel. The only drawback, they discovered, was when a rough relief barmaid was on duty. She refused to serve halves of draught beer and bullied customers into buying pints. She had ruled a tap room during her last job at a pub like a tyrant and thought she could do the same at the hotel. Not that she remained there long but her reign was provocative to say the least.

Handling their pint glasses with care and keeping a wary eye on Florrie's hefty stand-in, they moaned to themselves that they could not buy pints in the cocktail bar yet were coerced into buying them in the hotel's down-market saloon.

Their drinking world was becoming crazy, they decided before going over the details of the case. Then the duo met Joan in the cocktail bar where they bought halves that were as expensive as pints elsewhere.

"What are we going to do?" she asked, peering at their blank faces in dismay. "Well, obviously you are both lost but I have an idea. We could put a small, coded message in the personal column of the newspaper. It would not make sense to anyone except the man behind all this trouble. I am sure the Editor will go along with it."

Phil responded immediately: "The problem with that is the police could spot it and put two and two together. There's a sergeant who goes through the adverts in the newspaper every week looking for items and goods that have been stolen and then put for sale. He never misses an issue."

Joan was undeterred: "My other idea is to do with Peter."

"Peter?" the duo asked in dim unison.

"Yes, Ralph's mate, the Co-op's fast delivery boy, sorry youth. He knows everyone in the village of Gorton in more ways than one. We'll ask him to circulate a story in that wonderful human rumour machine that provides Ralph with most of his news leads - the legendary grapevine. Bad news travels fast and sensational news even faster. We'll plant a story announcing that another body has been found, and that the newspaper knows all about it. That will draw our criminal into a trap. Easy.

"The police won't pick-up on the rumour since they no longer have a village policeman there. Had Bobby Lee been alive, he would have heard the story before it left Peter's mouth. That won't happen these days.

"If Mary Elliott was wrong and there isn't a second body, then we'll just tell Peter to start another rumour saying the original one is not true. We can't lose."

"Oh, Ralph, darling, I'll have a martini, please, not smelly draught beer tonight, thank you. I deserve the best."

"Divine," she declared on taking a sip.

Peter's handsome dark looks brightened when told of the plan. Just up his street, said the Casanova of the estates, and by the time Ralph had left his home Peter was wondering who would be chosen to set off the tale which would spread like a virus around the terraced streets and council houses.

There was Mrs Robinson in Laker Street. She was in her 40s, had been married for years and knew everyone. Yes, he thought, she would be good. When told to keep gossip to herself it was soon whizzing along Gorton's longest street, and within two days the entire village knew.

What about Mrs Grainger in Whitworth Road? Plump, attractive and known as 'Mrs Week Before the Advertiser' given that she knew lots of news before it appeared in the newspaper. She was trustworthy and highly accurate, Peter concluded. Few of the rumours she heard were distorted or exaggerated on entering her lucid section of the grapevine.

As for Mrs Benson? He wasn't sure about her. Very communicative and a decent storyteller in the back yard and pub. She was shapely and that could be a problem since she might ask him for too many favours in return for using her as a cheap alternative to the General Post Office's telegram boy.

He went for Mrs Grainger who did not disappoint the team.

In that insular community where everyone's business was known by all, the plan ticked over as smoothly as the town hall clock. But the scribblers did not realise there had been a breakthrough for a few days on the grounds nothing appeared to happen on the surface. Not one clue or lead emerged.

Ralph had expected the phones in the office to start ringing almost immediately with new revelations and that the scam would lure the local criminals out of the shadows. It was all very simple. Once the guilty man appeared at the office or at another rendezvous, a lurking photographer would take a snatch photograph while Ralph and Phil engaged the criminal in a conversation. Meanwhile Joan would tip-off the police.

The callers on the office phones that day were the usual suspects, however, and mundane topics were on their minds: a family wanting to publicise a daughter having gained a university degree; a local councillor pressing for a story to be published about mining subsidence destroying growing numbers of homes and a man asking for the date of the annual Northfield Feast holiday so he could book a week for his family at a boarding house in Blackpool.

"What's happened?" asked Ralph after the

working day was over. Downcast and needing a pint of beer, he blamed his girlfriend.

"Joan's plan has backfired. Trust her. She's cocked it all up. There has been no response. I knew we should have printed an advert in the newspaper and flushed him out that way."

Phil remarked: "I think we were a little naïve, Ralph. He's a clever man who isn't going to fall for rumour that a group of gossips spread around his village."

Later the next day Joan, still recovering from the mental bruising inflicted on her by her lover, finished the last story of the day, tidied her desk, and said cheerio to everyone and descended the stairs to the ground floor. She waved to Susan in reception and left the building, heading down the hill to meet Ralph near the open market as they planned to watch a production of The King and I at the civic hall.

Life wasn't bad, she thought. After a Topsy-Turvey start she now liked the job and even relished her unconventional colleagues. What's more, she was in love. Ralph was growing on her.

Smiling to herself, her mind wandered to their forthcoming weekend in London. The itinerary, drawn up by them during a boozy evening in the cocktail bar, included long walks in the parks, high-class meals, and a night to remember at The Hilton.

But before their romantic weekend away she wanted to give him a special delight – a jolly good fright in her Sprite. She planned to sprint down a stretch of the A-1 near The Ram Jam Inn at 80mph and then laugh at the stupefied look on his face. The ride from hell would also make him more susceptible to her advances by removing defensive mechanisms that sometimes blocked his emotions, she quipped to close friends.

Bravo, they retorted. Give him hell.

Chapter 12

"Excuse me, young lady," … a car drew up alongside her as she walked to meet Ralph. Winding down the front passenger window, the driver, a grey-haired man in his 50s, leaned forward and smiled while he held a road map.

"Could you direct me to Kingstone?" he asked, pleadingly, his forehead sweating profusely. "I am in a hurry."

Always willing to help strangers in trouble, she paused and pondered but then a pedestrian's hand gripped her left arm, and a third man standing on the pavement behind her opened the rear door and pushed her headfirst onto the seat. Protesting fiercely and trying to wriggle free, she was horrified when a fist smashed in her face, and she was bluntly told to shut up or else.

So began a ride to hell, not down the A-1 with Ralph but to an unknown destination in Northfield with a gang of thugs.

Slumping semi-conscious onto the seat, she was held down by the two men who squeezed into the remaining space in the rear of the car. She was vaguely aware of watching a hazy image of the white

Portland stone town hall flashing past as the driver drove off at speed. Several bystanders witnessing the kidnapping waved to try to attract attention, screamed for the police, and pointed wildly at the rear of the car that was disappearing round the corner and into the town centre.

The driver glanced in his mirror and warned: "Do not move, do not say anything." By now her hands were tied behind her back, she was humiliatingly held face down and a nylon stocking was stuffed into her mouth so she could not reply even if she had wanted to do so.

"I bet this is the first time this woman has kept her pretty mouth shut for days," one of the men muttered. "You know what gabby women are like. The more they talk, the more they like it."

His companion, whose body odour was already beginning to irritate her nostrils, chipped in with: "I bet she likes it. Her boyfriend is very good looking, don't you think? I bet she's turbo-charged in bed."

The driver demanded: "Let's have a look at what she's got," and one of his pals pulled up her skirt to reveal her nylon stockings, suspender belt and underwear, all of which had been carefully selected by her to please Ralph in the privacy of the bedroom.

There was a bout of guttural male laughter and lewd comments as the car approached the outskirts of the town. The journey did not last long and involved a change of vehicles in a back yard or side street to throw the police off the scent.

It seemed like an eternity to Joan who was now

whimpering and praying for a miracle, and when they came to a halt, she had no idea where they were. A few minutes later the car was parked up at what she believed was their destination. She was bungled out of the vehicle, quickly blind-folded and led across what was thought to be a large garden. A few seconds later one of the men gripped her by the neck and she was forced into a building – it had a distinctive but not offensive rustic smell – and led down stone steps to a cellar, or that's what she thought at the time.

After she was forced to sit on the lone chair, the blindfold was removed, and her eyes took a few seconds to adjust to the poorly illuminated surroundings. Three heavily built men in balaclavas and overalls were standing there and she wondered in her despair whether she could withstand much more.

What were they going to do? What was this all about? Her mind was whirling but she still had enough mental discipline to realise her kidnapping had something to do with the Bobby Lee case. Having sensed a trap when the rumour went round the village, the thugs were not stupid enough to approach Ralph and Phil and instead waited for her leaving the office. The car must have been parked a few yards down the street from the office and as she emerged from the main entrance the slowly moving vehicle zeroed in on her from behind, with two accomplices walking alongside.

Finishing school and its sophisticated ways could not have prepared her for this plight, she thought, and for the first time in her life she was alone and terrified. Her hitherto dependable support system -her education, family, and social status – was absent and for a while she believed all that effort and money spent on her edification had been a waste of time.

The men, who had not uttered a word since the blindfold was removed, tied her to the chair and afterwards went out of the room, locked the door, and disappeared up the stone steps. Later a camp bed with blankets replaced the chair and she was permitted to sleep on it without her hands being tied. Slowly over the next few hours she gathered herself together and the family's celebrated internal steel bar, inherited from her self-made father, enabled her to come to terms with what was happening – for a while. Her hitherto all-consuming fear subsided.

She awoke the following day to find three hooded men standing together and staring at her. So garrulous during the abduction, they were now mute, and their eyes exhibited no emotion whatsoever. Their piercing gaze would have penetrated steel, she said later.

"What am I doing here?" she pleaded, the panic beginning to re-emerge. "What do you want from me? Money? My father has it? What right have you to keep me in this filthy hole? Who are you al

Later she shuddered in the darkness as she felt a mild tickling sensation on her ankle. It started to move slowly up her leg, clammy and creepy, and she screamed, lashing out with her leg to rid herself of this interloper. She threw off the blankets and got to her feet, extending her hand to reach out for the one electric switch in the room. The search seemed to take an eternity as she fumbled around the wall and, shaking, turned on the switch

All she saw was the scurrying of a rat as it shot across the floor and into a hole in the wall.

She sat down on the bed, took a deep breath, and did not weep, which was a good sign, she thought. It was imperative that she did not fall apart. But the light remained on for the rest of her incarceration and one of her shoes was kept handy in case the creature returned.

Over time her emotions performed somersaults, one minute she was weak, the next strong. Family ties and memories were deliberately revived to maintain order and discipline in her mind, but bouts of panic returned at random to scramble her thoughts. She wished she could alleviate the hell her parents must have been going through.

Wondering what Ralph was doing, she focused on the forthcoming weekend break in London and on all the wonderful things that were on their agenda. Life was so good before the nightmare, she assured herself. Now there was a strong possibility they would not meet again. On a couple of occasions she cried out and reprimanded herself for having taken him for granted since their relationship started four months earlier. Promising never to hurt him anymore, she prayed for her gallant knight to pull off a miracle and come to her rescue.

The following morning she was annoyed for having been so mawkish. Ralph, no longer the hero of her dreams, was pushed into the background in her mind, and she assessed the situation through the eyes of a hardnosed career woman, now emboldened to survive at all costs.

Gazing around the room, she shivered in the cold and never moaned to herself. She noted with disgust the filthy water dripping down one of the walls and the zoo of insects scurrying around the wooden floor, but she never cringed as she had done in the beginning.

Towards the end of her imprisonment there was even a glimpse of humour. One naked light bulb illuminated the room and despite her predicament she had sufficient clarity of mind to realise that at least the much-maligned lighting back in the office was marginally superior. That was the first and last time she smiled during her absence from Ralph.

On the evening of her disappearance he thought she may have been taken ill and was not too worried but became agitated on her failure to answer the phone at the flat. On arriving home, puzzled, he was confronted by his father who said a note was pushed into the letterbox that evening. Believing it was an inconsequential news item sent in for publication, probably written by a neighbour, he opened the envelope, and the contents were startling. It was a ransom note. First, he was told not to tell the police and then there was a demand for £20,000 for her safe return. A similar letter was sent to her father.

A few minutes later the phone rang. The caller was her father who was spitting fire, demanding to know why his daughter was put in the ridiculous firing line by management and threatening all kinds of retribution on the parochial hyenas in the office. That included poor Ralph. All chances of an engagement and marriage were now torpedoed, he concluded bitterly.

The following morning, asked by Don why Joan was not at work, he lied and said she had been called away to look after a sick relative, adding her father, Brian, would back him up.

"I wish you young people would realise you are supposed to ring in in person when taking time off through illness," added Don, nettled by what he thought was the easy-going manner of a post war lost generation of idlers and hedonists.

Having confided in Phil, his mentor, the two reporters tried to figure out the identity of the kidnapper and the consensus was Gerald James, the farmer, whose name was on the list of suspects being examined by the police.

"I do not understand it," said Phil, "why have the police not done anything about him? In the old days the detectives would have knocked him around until he told the truth. Have you seen this...?"

Ralph was handed a copy of that evening's late edition of the Sheffield Star. The lead story on the front page screamed: "Woman snatched by gang in Northfield drama." The story stated the police were appealing for information since her abductors were unknown and the long columns of type were full of eye-witness accounts and graphic descriptions of what had happened.

Phil added: "Eric Richards, their reporter, made a good job of the material he had, and we could have added a lot more facts to give our story some pace, but thanks to you we must keep our mouths shut."

Ralph was angry: "I am pining deeply for my missing girl; on second thoughts I am distraught and all you can say is that Eric made a good job of the facts. That's diabolical, insensitive on your part. I thought you were a mate. Get lost!

"Anyway, the story is not 100 per cent correct."

Phil, puzzled, replied: "The report looks okay to me."

Ralph: "Not to me. Eric says she was abducted in Market Hill. Wrong. It happened 20 yards farther away in Church Street. Different street. So there."

Phil: "You are being too picky. It's not a titanic mistake, is it? They are basically the same street; one runs into the other. The information came from the police and Eric repeated it. Nothing wrong with that. The police should get it right in the first place.

"That does not change the fact that you'll get into serious trouble if you do not say something to the police soon. We have perverted the course of justice and withheld vital evidence. A serious crime if you can recall your tuition in newspaper law and you could get a jail sentence if the judge has a bad night before the hearing. Not worth it; love that is. Not worth spending years in a police cell for a woman."

That night Ralph went through his own sequence of nightmares. As tenacious as ever he fought his own imaginary demons that were trying to monopolise his sleep and in the morning he was emotionally exhausted. Preparing to drag himself to work, he thought of one person – Joan.

A week went by and still Ralph had not heard anything. Was Joan alive? Her father was seen by colleagues leaving the bank in Northfield with a briefcase – which Ralph assumed was full of cash – and both fearful families sat back to see what happened.

Two days later Ralph answered the door during a rainy evening to confront a wet and bedraggled Joan standing on the doorstep. Both burst into tears and hugged each other until they ached.

"I can't stay," she said, wiping the rain and tears from her face. "They released me two hours ago and father picked me up. He wasn't enamoured with the idea of coming here. You are not his favourite person. But I had to see you. Don knows what's happened and we have a second round of interviews with the police tomorrow. I won't be at work for a few days.

"I think I was held captive at a farmhouse. There was a pleasant agricultural smell about the place, reminded me of one of my aunt's farms in Lancashire but everything else over the last few days has been awful. It's marvellous that I've managed to survive, and dad did not hesitate when paying the ransom despite contradictory advice from the police. I'll have to go."

She clutched his hand and said: "The thought of you kept me going. Love you."

Ralph, trembling with joy, waved as she crossed the street and slid into the front passenger seat of her father's Jaguar.

On returning to work she wrote a series of news stories and features on her ordeal underground and caused a sensation, not only locally but nationwide. She was interviewed on regional television and radio and the journalists from the national newspapers hounded her for days. The job offers came tumbling in and that's when she started to evolve into a stranger.

A change in her demeanour in the office was noted. She became standoffish and reluctant to spend time with him. His presence was resented, and she preferred to talk to colleagues whom she had politely ignored in the past. He ignored all the tell-tale signs, not having realised what was happening to their imploding world.

On striding into the cocktail bar one evening he gave Betty one of his ear-to-ear grins, asking her to hippy hippy shake the mixer. The patrons were in awe as she rattled and rolled the stainless-steel cylinder to produce two exquisite cocktails.

He paid for the drinks without his usual hesitation and slumped into an easy chair. Joan sat opposite him with her glass and smiled weakly; she couldn't take her eyes off him as she was preparing to announce bad news.

"Betty is the best shaker in the world," Ralph declared, sipping the cherished blend of gin and Vermouth, complete with ice and the inevitable cherry. "This is wonderful. Never had one while you were away. I couldn't drink alcohol; went right off it. I wanted to save the pleasure of downing this nectar for your big welcome back into this world."

He was in the mood to dip into his voluminous collection of quirky tales: "Did you know that Dorothy Parker once said that she liked to have a martini? Two were delicious. After three she was under the table, after four under the host. That's a good one, isn't it?"

"Who is Dorothy Parker?" answered Joan, glumly.

"Where were you educated, Joan?" he answered, annoyed his story had failed to arouse mirth.

"You are supposed to say something like: 'I'll have three more –your name must be Mr Host'. Get it?"

"Not tonight, darling; I am not in the mood."

Betty, embarrassed by the chilly silence developing between the couple, interjected: "I know who she was. A witty writer who knocked out articles for fancy intellectual magazines in New York."

"Well done, Betty," he added. "At least one person is well read."

"Where did you go to school?"

"Northfield Secondary Modern School," she said, embarrassed.

"Think yourself lucky as Joan went to finishing school in the Alps," he said, laughing. "Fancy not knowing about Dorothy Parker."

Unperturbed, Joan sipped her drink, but her mind

was not in the room, and she was first sombre and then moody. He did not take much notice since he thought it was something to do with a gruelling reaction to what she had been through.

Betty, however, was anything but moody. She was elated since she enjoyed being described as the best cocktail shaker in the world and, surprisingly, at least one person thought she was so well read. Anyway she had been fancying Ralph for ages while working in one of the hotel's downbeat bars frequented by him and his beery mates. His presence made her happy.

Finally, Joan lassoed enough courage to broach what was on her mind but even then she couldn't go through with an insensitive announcement that would lead to a monumental upheaval in their lives. "I have something to say, Ralph, but not here. What's on my mind is too personal. We'll have to go back to the flat."

Betty, whose sharp hearing could pick-up conversations at the other end of the room, realised what was unfolding. She glanced knowingly and lovingly at Ralph who was still in denial when it came to Joan.

Back in the flat she made two coffees and then, reluctantly, told him she had accepted a lucrative job on a newspaper in London. It was too good to miss, and she was planning to leave Northfield within days, ignoring the requirement to serve two weeks' notice. Her father proposed to buy her an apartment in the capital.

His face failed to react to the news but inside his emotions collapsed. He remained silent for a few minutes, staring at his now former lover, and then rose awkwardly from the chair, his mind partially fogged by the alcohol. He walked out of the flat without a word. Joan, sobbing out of deeply felt guilt, knew she had done the best thing, however. Northfield, thankfully, was slowly receding out of her life.

"You can't make omelettes without breaking eggs," her mother said later, relieved she had jettisoned a small-town reporter with no ambition. "Your father and I have been worried about your relationship with that man for a long time."

Chapter 13

The following morning Don was bad tempered as he waved Joan's resignation letter in the office and vowed to take legal action for breach of contract, but everyone knew he wouldn't do anything. Ralph's sorrowful expression told him the relationship with Joan was over.

"Oh, I am sorry to interrupt your grieving," he announced, cruelly, "but the police want to see you. Had a phone call 20 minutes ago. You'll probably be in clink for 1,000 years."

The police inspector was reclining casually in his chair behind the desk on the top storey of the police station. Both men did not like each other.

"Before I get down to the serious stuff involving your refusal to help the police when your sexy pal was kidnapped, I'll tell you what happened after her father had dropped off the money to the kidnappers. She was blindfolded, taken out of her prison, and dumped on a playing field in Northfield. That's where dad collected her and both went home.

"We have searched the tunnels and under the floorboards of the bunker; your informant was correct as we have discovered more human remains. As you are probably aware the police have no idea who was behind the kidnapping or the earlier killings."

Ralph looked at him surprised since Gerald James, the farmer, whose name was on the list of suspects, must have been culpable, according to the available evidence. But the policeman said he had been exonerated and had water-tight alibis. Other suspects were checked out as well, all of whom appeared to be innocent.

"Joan said she was incarcerated in what appeared to be the cellar of a farmhouse," said Ralph. "The place had the smell of a farm. Isn't that good enough to interview James again? We have been thinking he was the villain for ages."

The policeman added: "James was seriously ill in hospital for a few days while your lady friend was in the cellar. We were also watching him for days afterwards and our officers reported there was nothing unusual about his activities. Forget that line of enquiry. What's suddenly made you act like Sherlock Holmes?"

He added:" On top of that shambles surrounding her disappearance, we are still baffled by the disappearance of P.c Lee 20 years ago. So, as you can see, we have not been doing a very thorough job. But do not quote me or else."

Grinning sardonically, he looked straight into Ralph's eyes: "If you do go against our wishes, then I'll go hell for leather and get you charged with hampering police enquiries about your missing girlfriend."

He laughed again: "Sorry, she's no longer your girlfriend, is she? Shame. Bad news gets around in a small town. But that's how it pans out these days - nothing lasts forever. Now get lost. Our prosecution department will assess whether you'll be charged along with that oversexed pal of yours, Phil. I do not like him either."

Joan never returned to work at the Advertiser and instead prepared for her move south. Within a week she decamped to London but not before meeting Ralph for a farewell coffee in a local café.

"I do not like what I am doing," she said bluntly. "But I cannot stay here. Every time I went past Two Trees, I would think of Miss Elliott and have a nervous breakdown. My experience underground in that other hell hole was horrifying. I can't flee fast enough.

"Just one thing. It may come in useful in the future. One of the few things I remember from my ordeal is one of them had a cast in one of his eyes. He could well have been the driver of the car but I'm not sure. For some inexplicable reason I did not mention his defect to the police. Odd that. But I am not going back to tell them. Perhaps I need to track the villain down myself, long into the future when I have calmed down.

"As far as work was concerned, I never belonged in the hallowed offices at the Advertiser. I can write long articles on Shakespeare's works and the music of Bach, but I do not know what happens in the next street to my house. The local stuff is what's important to the newspaper, not the dry material studied at university.

"You are a natural news gatherer. Don says you have a talent for ferreting out news items. Good ones. I do not know how you found all those wonderful human-interest stories. Can you remember going into The Butchers' pub and finding a guy standing at the bar who was having a quiet pint of beer? Looked like the average man from Northfield. But he had just returned from Hong Kong where he had overseen hundreds of coolies on behalf of the Royal Navy and was now enjoying retirement in his hometown.

"You did a great story and the following week after publication his old shipmate living in Northfield wrote in stating they had last met serving on a gunboat 1,000 miles up China's Yangtze River 40 years earlier. You arranged a reunion, and they had a splendid time. You can't make that kind of story up. You have a knack. You'll always find something that is quirky and bubbling away under the surface.

"Yet, in contrast, I couldn't get my head round the rest of our news. It's parish pump material, both monumentally absurd and meaningless to anyone living beyond Northfield and I belong in Fleet Street. I need wider horizons, banner headlines, exhilaration and a lifestyle to match."

Ralph could not hide his feelings any longer and tried to grasp her hand as they sat across from each other at the table in The Aloha coffee bar. She withdrew it swiftly as if touched by that rat in the cellar.

"Do not start that," she muttered, giving him a toxic look. "Not here. I am serious; I do not want anything to do with you. It's finished, get it?"

Ralph: "I do not understand. On the day you were released by the gang you said I was your shining light during the imprisonment. You loved me. What happened? The change in your attitude has been so dramatic."

Leaning back in her chair, she glanced around to see if anyone was listening and gave him a hard look.

"To tell the truth I am not entirely sure myself. I have been traumatised, perhaps brutalised, that's all I know. My feelings shut down when I returned to my parents' home. The portcullis came down with a bang. Since then, I feel cold inside and have no feelings for you at all. Or for anyone else. I doubt whether I'll be in love again, so I'll pour everything into my profession and make a name for myself. "

Her austere expression relaxed, and she continued: "I have fond memories of our time together. Those walks were good. I always thought until then that you had to travel to the south of France or taste nightlife in London to enjoy yourself. We went down that lane so many times the farmer got to know us and waved while working in the fields.

"Can you recall when it rained and we ran to shelter in his barn, and he laughed? I think farmers enjoy the rain. I'll never forgot and when I meet you again in ten years or so, I'll recall our times together and look at your reaction. I'll also remember with fondness our evenings and nights in my flat. You may well be married to a dreadful hectoring woman with three screaming children and our time together won't mean anything to you.

"I think we were too young for a big relationship. There was no protective wall to shield our emotions from the colossal stuff. Our affair was fun but could not survive that brutal imprisonment I had to endure. Perhaps there will be a second time around in a few years. Who knows.

"Haven't you anything to say?"

"Not really, "he answered, now realising their affair was a lost cause but the ache inside continued to be raw for months. Like all journalists he was a competent actor and hid his feelings well.

"There has been some news at the office. Big news," he declared with a blank face – but his eyes twinkled with humour.

She was ensnared in the trap; not all his charm had vanished, and she retained a flicker of warmth towards him. "What's that?"

"Well, you'll be glad to know that the old naked electric light bulbs are being replaced with modern strip lighting and that we are getting several new Olivetti typewriters. Modern, lightweight and almost noiseless. Your old machine with its heavy, stubbornly defiant keys that flattened fingertips is going to the scrapyard. Oh, I have forgotten, new carpets have been ordered as well.

"Had I known, I would have stayed," she joked, but her attempt at humour failed. Rising from her chair, she gave him a loveless kiss on the cheek, said goodbye without any hint of emotion and walked out of the café, leaving a defeated young man at the table.

It was lunchtime on Christmas Eve and Don was having a festive pint with several members of his staff in Florrie's bar.

"What a year!" he moaned. His colleagues smiled to themselves and glanced at each other; good old Don was his usual morbid self at Christmas.

"I am reviewing our glorious year for your benefit. Our ace reporter was kidnapped and held for ransom, then fled to London for more money; her dreamboat is so cut up he is incapable of doing any work save rewriting St Mary's Parish Church magazine and Phil has gone to our arch-rivals for a large wage packet. At least we are going to get the office carpeted, fitted carpet at that, and fabulous new lighting. Roll in 1966. Whoopee! We may get a short-wave radio so we can zero into police messages.

"What's that dreadful noise emanating from the jukebox?"

"The Beatles," came the reply.

"Oh them," answered Don. "In a couple of years, they'll be forgotten. Contemporary rubbish – no staying power. I bet you did not know the local cricket lovers' society were planning on having The Beatles to provide the music at their annual dance three years ago. The committee had never heard of them and booked a big band instead. Now that's good music. Like Sinatra's songs. What a crooner."

There was no customary tittering, so he looked round; his staff had gone – to the next pub.

Don was always correct with his forecasts except when it came to music.

Part 2
Chapter 14
The year, 1972

Big Ben was booming in the background when Ralph lifted the receiver of his office phone, and he realised immediately that Mark Pinder, junior, the newly elected MP for the Northfield constituency, was preparing to speak from his office in Westminster.

"Hello, Ralph, how are you?"

That question would be heard by the reporter many times over the ensuing years, at times inflamed by anger, Mark having been infuriated by a critical editorial in the newspaper, and at times sprinkled with laughter or respect. It was all part of the great game of politics and newspapers, and both men became adept at manipulating each other.

The politician had done well in the traditional sense. He had worked hard as a miner and brought up three children. At the same time he had followed the official line in the miners' union, rising in its ranks without creating ripples and after a few years was elected a councillor to gain experience in the local corridors of power. When the opportunity arose

118

following the death of the MP, he was selected as the parliamentary candidate for the solid Labour constituency in the general election and was elected with a large majority.

Old King Coal dominated the town. The miners' union, with its enormous membership, had more delegates eligible to vote at Labour Party meetings than all the other trade unions and party branches put together. As a result their members were always selected as prospective parliamentary candidates: he had walked down a well-trodden and successful political path to parliament.

"I have to thank you for all your support with my news coverage in the Advertiser," said Mark. "Long may it last. You'll have to come here sometime, have a few drinks in the bars – this place is a revelation. A few years ago I was eating dust underground and listening to the groaning of the coal seams and the moaning of the men. We sweated our way through every shift, every week - this lot down here do not know what hard work is.

"Talking about hard work, how are you progressing, Ralph? You work too hard, you know. Still thinking of that old girlfriend. What was her name? Joan?"

She was long gone, and Ralph was replicating what she had pledged to do in London, submerging himself into the job. Girlfriends were no longer on the radar. No one in the office ever mentioned the journalist from finishing school who caused anarchy in the town.

Nor did the reporters talk about the mysterious death of Bobby Lee. The latter story was destined to remain in the yellowing newspaper files in the office cellar. Even Don, clinging to the job while young tearaways looking for promotion harassed the routine and challenged decisions made in the office, had something else on his mind – survival in a cut-throat business.

Mark added: "I have got something to tell you, Ralph. A tip. There's a nationwide miners' strike brewing. It's coming fast and no-one in your industry seems to realise what's happening. It's the first for nearly 50 years. In 1926 we got a drumming but I'm not sure that will happen these days. It's 1972 and the nation depends too much on coal. The power stations have a colossal hunger for it, and we'll hold the government to ransom. We'll halt supplies of the fuel to power stations and industry. Close the country down. Our young 'uns want to put the clog in.

"You need to build contacts and find a young and daring miners' union official to supply inside information. The old union leaders at the Yorkshire headquarters in Barnsley are too old and complacent. They'll get swept away in the avalanche following the dispute. I'll give you the names of a couple of potential contacts who'll probably step in as our union leaders after it's all over. Out with the old, in with the new and the union will open a new chapter in its history.

He added: "Catch me if you can."

Ralph asked: "What's all that about?"

Laughing, Mark commented: "It's my grandfather's old phrase. He was involved in the 1926 miners' dispute. He was an unofficial union liaison man between the leaders and miners in the coalfields. He never used his real name on field work; instead, the phrase was printed on cards sent to his union contacts and thereby they knew who was coming to see them. You never knew who friend or foe was in those days – there could have been someone in the union in the pay of the police. So, if you get that message on a card at some time in the future, you'll know who it is – me."

Ralph: "You know, I have heard those words before. Not sure where. A small bell from a long time ago is ringing away in my brain. It will come back. There was a Dave Clark Five hit in the 1960s called Catch Us If You Can but that's not the connection."

After the strike kicked-in, Ralph met his union contact in Florrie's emporium, a long dark bar where there were no eavesdroppers or CID officers. The mainly Irish clientele continued to down pints and talk treason in a light-hearted fashion while half listening to the ageing Beatles' records on the highly illuminated jukebox.

Everything about the place was old fashioned, but management had made one concession in the name of progress: sawdust was no longer used to soak-up spilled beer or dubious liquid-like substances deposited on the floorboards. Buckets and mops were now the preferred panacea in such circumstances.

Frank, a union branch official, was gaunt with

thick black hair and, like a lot of miners, was physically fit but on the small side. Ralph noticed there was not an inch of flab on his stomach and the handshake was vice-like, the trademark of a working miner.

During the strike he never leaked anything highly confidential from the union but provided background information and quirky titbits of news to keep Ralph and the Editor happy. All went well until a puzzled Frank arrived at the bar to tell the reporter something odd was happening on the picket lines. From the union's point of view the situation was going well and the power stations were struggling as supplies of coal were interrupted or cut-off by pickets.

"But we are getting back reports that are beginning to worry us," he grumbled. "The police appear to have inside information. We have sent out pickets on back roads, but police cars have been waiting and turned them back. It's worrying our leaders. There is a spy in the camp."

Ralph: "Who do you think it is? The information to the police could have come from leaks in the NCB. Half the personnel officers at the pits are ex-union men who have gone over to the other side and perhaps several harbour old loyalties. They have retained unofficial contact with union sources. Your problem is that your men do not have much sympathy with the rest of the nation's population."

The meetings between them continued for the rest of the dispute – though the spy was never discussed again - and Ralph compiled his news reports on what he was told and then juggled that material with the statements issued by the National Coal Board.

Often it was almost impossible to find a middle road between the two contradictory versions of what was supposed to be happening. As a result the newspaper received complaints from both sides that reporters were biased against them, which the Editor declared was reassuring on the grounds it convinced him his staff were doing their job.

One evening Frank was drinking by himself in the bar. Florrie, a pint-sized and elderly barmaid, was clamping down on a bout of rowdy behaviour by giving the ringleader a sharp look and a full-frontal view of one of her intimidating fingers.

"Are you watching Florrie's magical touch?" asked Ralph on arrival. "Quite a performance, isn't it? She's declined, unfortunately, with age but still formidable. I have seen burly men reduced to red-faced little boys by our little Florrie."

Frank bought him a pint of beer and then asked whether there were any sympathetic contacts on the staff of a national newspaper since he thought the union needed a touch of sound public relations - the miners' case for more money was not getting through to the public.

"I'll see what I can do," added Ralph, who later asked The Daily Mirror whether they could send one of their writers to the coalfield to talk to Frank and to various handpicked mining families. Their news editor's reply on the phone stunned him. Ralph, for once, was caught napping: the London journalist's bewildering answer was nothing to do with the strike or even politics.

"We have got the ideal candidate for the job," added the news editor, and he was laughing gently under his breath. "Our journalist insists you take her to Florrie's bar or whatever they call it. Florrie? There can't be such a bar in 1972! Is there? It's so old fashioned. Surely it must be The King's Arms or The Mojo these days. A swinging place with a fancy name. Perhaps not. Not in the barbaric, toothless north. Never been there but then it's had a bad press.

"Oh, before I forget, how is the old desk going in your office? Has it burst into flames yet? It belongs to Don, doesn't it?"

"How do you know about that in London?" stuttered Ralph, astonished. "This is out of order. Don will go mad if he hears about this. He's living in blissful ignorance about the twilight goings on in the office."

The London journalist laughed and added: "One of your former reporters works for us now. He took his girlfriends into your office at night and the stories have run rampant in Fleet Street. You lot oop north get all the fun."

"How do you know Don?" asked Ralph, still struggling to come to terms with the revelations.

"He worked down here for a time but missed the north. He resigned and went home. Said he had coal dust in his blood."

Having recovered from the shock that the love desk was now common knowledge in newspaper circles, he realised Joan was on her way home. Who else knew about Florrie's bar? He put down the phone and walked away in despair. On arrival a few days later she booked into the Queens, still regarded as the best hotel in town.

The high-flying journalist had been living in a world of luxury hotels for a few years and thought the old place had gone downhill in her absence; but for nostalgia's sake she took a quick look in the cocktail bar and then contacted Ralph by phone. His initial reaction was frosty but gradually her warmth and calculated persuasive manner wore him down and soon they were talking like old friends.

"Come on, Ralph, let's go to Florrie's bar. About time I met the old buzzard and then I'll get down to work. I hope you have lined up some decent contacts and we'll look after you with a generous tip-off fee. But let's get an update on what you have been doing. By the way, I drink beer these days, not cocktails. Journalism is a great leveller."

Florrie wasn't on duty that day and Betty was standing in. She greeted the new arrival coolly but thanks to their outgoing personalities they were soon chatting about fashion and other girlie topics and Ralph became an outcast until Frank's arrival. For the next two days Joan hoovered up all she could find on how miners' wives were coping during the strike while Ralph looked on with the kind of palpable pride that a mentor exhibits when an ex-pupil – and in his case ex- lover – reaches the pinnacle of their profession.

The inevitable did happen, however. For one evening during her brief stay they had a celebratory drink in the cocktail bar, where the conversation focused on their past life in Northfield, though her horrific experience underground was never mentioned. The past never goes away, concluded Ralph, and Joan soon relaxed and according to Betty there was a warmth in her eyes that did not exist on arrival from London.

"Joan, I am glad you came back," he said after a couple of hours in the bar, trying to control his emotions. "I wasn't looking forward to your visit but now I am happy. Very much so."

She glanced at the floor. Politely turning her back on Betty, she added: "So am I."

"Look, Ralph, the family continue to have connections with the flat in Northfield. Why don't we go home? Like old times."

Betty was the only person in the bar who wasn't pleased with their departure. She had gone out with him on a few occasions after Joan's great escape from Northfield years earlier but nothing long term had materialised. It was not true that everything came to the one who waited, she decided, and went back to shaking and rolling her stainless-steel mixer while the two former lovers walked out and headed towards the flat.

The following day Joan returned to London to continue her stellar career while he fossilized at the humble Advertiser. But not before they had an intimate farewell on the railway station at Doncaster, an event in marked contrast to the soulless goodbye last time around. Both wondered whether they would see each other again but did not dwell on the matter as their lives were following separate trajectories.

Chapter 15

"Guess what's happened?" asked Don a couple of weeks later. He was now looking forward to retirement – even though it was years away - but one day his personality suddenly brightened on answering the phone in the office. Ralph looked at his beaming face, concluding something intriguing was galloping out of the history books.

"I was thinking that filling the newspaper these days could be difficult since the end of the miners' strike, but I was wrong," trumpeted Don. "Ralph, what have a couple of trees and a doctor in common? Come on, it monopolised your teenage years. One of the great mysteries of our time. Perhaps I ought to mention the name Joan and an abduction. There is someone waiting in reception for you – you have suddenly become famous."

Ralph: "Bobby Lee? Good grief has that come back like a nasty burp? What's happened? It's not Mary Elliott, is it?"

Bobby Lee's son, now middle aged, was sitting in reception waiting for Ralph to arrive and the inevitable question: "Can we go somewhere private?" was already trembling in anticipation on the visitor's nervous lips. The son, Derek, did not waste the reporter's time.

Ensconced in the room reserved for interviews, Derek spilled out the results of 15 years of investigations into his father's death.

"I got interested in my late teens," he said. "The police never seemed to do a decent job to find the culprit and several of my father's former colleagues have said there was corruption in the force in the old days: names and witness statements often went missing. I realise you know about that so-called list of shame which included the names of people involved in the black market. I believe that was a decoy. They were small fish. Even men with no connection with the gang were on the list.

"My mother said before her death that dad was involved and took cash on the side to give me a decent childhood during the hard days in the war. She kept her mouth shut until the very end when she needed to clear her conscience.

"The names on the list were scrutinised by the police and nothing untoward could be found on the men who were still alive. The real boss man was not among the names. He was from Manchester, a member of one of their notorious gangs, and he came over to Gorton to take over command. Commuted between Manchester and the village by rail and few people knew him.

"There was something strange about the village in those days. It was a deferential community, but the residents' loyalty was wasted on the wrong people.

"They turned a blind eye to Miss Elliott's misdemeanours as she squirrelled away the ill-gotten gains and squandered the lot on dinners, soirees and charity. No-one knew for certain what she was up to, but they had a good idea and kept quiet. Something nasty seemed to be at work there. She pulled the levers in the village and virtually paid the inhabitants hush money through her charity work.

"It was the same with the black-market gang. Many knew what was happening but did not spill the beans. One or two locals may have tipped off the police but my father, who had the gift of the gab, would have found a way of burying the complaints in the system so no action against the gang was taken. It is difficult to quantify the villagers' behaviour. They were on the surface decent people. However, I think in both instances they were getting something for nothing, i.e. a scout hut, free Christmas functions for pensioners and cheap cigs and booze. So they kept their lips zipped up.

"There was malice in every section of that community. From top to bottom. That's why Miss Elliott and the black marketeers flourished like weeds. Money and power corrupt, but so does overripe camaraderie. That gives people the idea they can get away with crime, even murder. The much-vaunted term close-knit community has a dark side to it.

"As far as I can ascertain, having spoken in my early enquiries to father's ex-colleagues, my father became greedy, threatened to expose the gang, and was murdered by them in a perfect place, the secret bunker where his remains were not discovered for 20 years. It was a classic crime. The other guy who was killed must have run afoul of our villains as well."

Ralph replied: "But who was the Godfather?"

Derek responded: "He was called Brian Davies. He returned to Manchester full-time once the income from black-market goods evaporated at the end of the war and remained there until his death in the 1950s."

Puzzled, Ralph continued: "That doesn't explain why I was beaten up in the 1960s. Or for trying to establish what happened to your father or why my girlfriend of the time was kidnapped and held for a week somewhere until her father produced a substantial ransom."

Derek realised his next revelation would throw a firecracker into the interview.

"Do you know someone called Pinder?"

Ralph's face dropped: "You mean the MP? Yes, of course I do. Everyone knows Mark. He can't have had anything to do with the gang – he was a mere lad during the war. His trade union and political life didn't really take off until the 1960s."

Derek: "He may well be innocent, but his uncle was a member of the mob."

"Good grief. Where did he fit in? How do you know all this? I realise some of the material has come from ex-members of the gang as well as from old police sources. But where else?"

Derek: "One of the old thugs kept a diary, a detailed one. I got it off his daughter for a few pounds.

It covered the war years, went into detail about where the whiskey, cigs and nylon stockings came from – mainly nicked in Lancashire – and whereabouts the mob stored the contraband, in the tunnels at Two Trees. Also, the diary included the names of people – many of whom were respectable individuals – who bought the stuff.

"The name Pinder kept coming up on the pages. He was the knuckle man. A rather nasty individual who was nevertheless popular and who knew what was going off in the village. He had links in every street. He was still a force of nature even in the 1960s.

"I reckon he was the one who was responsible for beating you up, killing the two men in the bunker and for kidnapping the girl. He vanished and we later learned he was in Spain in the late 1960s and therefore must have had an avalanche of money from somewhere. The ransom paid for his fancy lifestyle in the sun. You ought to know he's back in Gorton. I think he's had a severe stroke and came back to be treated on our incredible national health service."

Ralph: "Did he have a cast in one of his eyes by any chance?"

"He does. How do you know that?"

"The ex-girlfriend told me. It was one of the few things she remembered about her ordeal."

Like Don, Ralph, having been in the job a few years, was now capable of using his long memory.

"You know old Mary Elliott once warned me about the Pinder family. I did not believe her. Just thought she was nuts and had a grudge against the

Pinders. Well, well. So James the farmer was a decoy? We all thought he was guilty. Even Joan believed he was involved but she was misled by her father who I think was involved with the gang in the old days.

"What about those three names, including James, that appeared on Jimmy's list? If they were innocent, what was the point of keeping that piece of paper for all those years? It was even locked away in a solicitor's safe for a while. I wasted a lot of time trying to nail those men."

"It was just another bit of deception," Derek replied. "In this case by Jimmy's father. In the event of a police investigation, he wanted to divert attention to men who were not innocent but who were not the top men. The investigation never took place after the war and the list languished in a box in the wardrobe."

Ralph: "I thought most of the men earmarked for a life in the bunker were soldiers. Where did the black marketers and locals come in?"

Derek: "All but two or three were highly skilled soldiers, the type who today would be in the SAS. The irregulars lived in the locality. Local knowledge was essential. The squad did not want to blow up the local police station rather than the Gestapo headquarters two doors away. You get the drift?

"Pinder knew one of the bunker's specialists in explosives from his days in the army in the 1930s. He gave Pinder one of the special keys for the bunker's exit into the grounds at Two Trees. I do not know why. Perhaps Pinder was a blackmailer as well as a thug.

"At the beginning of the war the full squad spent periods in the bunker preparing the place for the expected invasion. As the war went on the visits became infrequent on the grounds that the threat became less likely. The government inspectors paid fewer calls as well. By the end of the war the place was almost derelict, but it served the marketeers well.

"Pinder must have had a field day. The black marketeers were given a free rein by him. The house and grounds were shielded from public gaze by rows of densely planted trees and Miss Elliott, afraid her own secret could be exposed by official interference, kept quiet.

Ralph added: "Are you going to the police with your file? Surely you want to try to avenge your father?"

Derek: "It was all a long time ago. I set off with that intention, determined to find what happened to my father. It was an obsession. When I was young my father had a large halo, a god in my eyes. The more I discovered the more my dreams were shattered. Now I have got this far I am not going anyway near the police.

"I'm going to walk away. I spent so many years thinking he was innocent. How wrong I was."

His eyes searched his interviewer's face for a reaction, but Ralph did not oblige.

"You know, Ralph. One day you may do the same. You'll set off to accomplish something, work hard and on the point of realising your dream you'll walk away. It's the easy thing to do."

Ralph, shaking his head, replied: "I do not think so."

Derek concluded: "You have just seen me self-destruct during this interview."

"What do you mean by that?"

"Never mind. Perhaps you will find out shortly. You can use all my material about the riddle of Two Trees; I do not care anymore."

He finished the interview with a warning: "I know the MP is a friendly man who does good deeds, but he is a Pinder. Be careful, Ralph."

Don read Ralph's latest stories about the case, concluding with a grin: "The old stories are always the best. This one never ends. Turns up every few years like the black sheep of the family."

Ralph went into detail about what had happened all those years ago. Hammering out the story on his Olivetti electric typewriter, the latest novelty in the office, he wished Joan was sitting next to him. She was guaranteed to produce a pertinent word that fitted well into the narrative of any story, and she had the skill to draw inspiration out of him when his creativity was on the point of ebbing.

He recalled with affection the times at her flat, the long spells of enjoyable silence and stillness that comes from kindred spirits. At the same time the couple recharged their batteries in the flat in preparation for bursts of typing and stress the following day. Their closeness in those days was remarkable, he believed, and could not fully understand why she had broken the bond and fled south.

After deliberations with Don and the Editor, an expert on newspaper law, he published the name of the Godfather, Brian Davies, since he was dead and therefore could not be libelled. He refrained from using the name Pinder, who was still alive, for legal reasons. He never outlined his uncle's nefarious life to the sitting MP and never approached Joan with the new disclosures. Not that she would have been bothered at that stage of her career. She was learning a new job – as the New York correspondent with a quality London newspaper.

His story almost wrapped up the old mystery of Two Trees. But who had pulled the trigger in both cases? That would remain a mystery. He did not fancy brutally interrogating an old man over an ancient case. He was going soft, he believed, and perhaps that was a good thing for the benefit of his long-term mental health.

Publication of the interview with Derek saw scores of extra newspapers sold at newsagents. Most of the readers devoured the revelation but there were one or two who complained the Advertiser was becoming like the News of the World, too sensational for its own good. Some regular orders were cancelled by uptight and upright readers.

"You ought to be ashamed of yourself, Ralph," the Vicar, the Rev F.L.R. Jones, commented one day. "It's gutter journalism and does not sit well in a newspaper of record. It all happened decades ago.

What relevance has it to events today?"

Where's he been for the last 50 years? wondered Ralph, who was hurt that someone deemed a friend was capable of being so cutting. Then he recalled that one of the articles left out of the newspaper to provide extra space for the story of the decade was Mr Jones's weekly column. Dennis, one of the new reporters, said Mr Jones's literary contribution was the most soporific item he had ever read until he had seen Don's latest Onlooker column, which he believed was as dry as the human dust at the crematorium.

Meanwhile, the police made a feeble attempt at reopening the cold case, Derek disappeared, and his body was later fished out of the Irish sea. The police concluded the man, depressed by his revelations about his father and the recent death of his beloved mother, had committed suicide.

Ralph submitted much of the evidence to the police but never mentioned Pinder, perhaps in misguided loyalty to his political friend, and he also realised with a shiver that one day Joan would want to track down her abductor.

Chapter 16
The year, 1983

The newspaper was again handling spectacular news. The nation's coal mines were speeding towards another big one – a nationwide strike - and both combatants, the National Coal Board and the miners' union, were playing malicious games.

The reporters, bombarded with facts and half-truths from the protagonists, handled their stories with care and their contacts with even more care. One false move and Ralph would not only lose a source of information but a friend, such as Frank, the union man who was a contact during the 1972 dispute. He always remained loyal to the newspaperman and often soaked up the flak from his anti-media comrades when they thought Ralph had blundered big time by writing a story which they thought had rattled the union cage.

Both men now made contact at The Penny Farthing, the erstwhile Florrie's Bar, the last vestiges of which had been swept aside in an expensive refurbishment. The highly illuminated jukebox and its collection of old Beatles' records was ejected, along with the old beer pumps that seemed to groan in protest when pulled.

For the first time in its history the 70-year-old floor was expensively carpeted, and richly upholstered seats were strategically placed around the room, the new look providing a welcome haven for smartly dressed people with a few quid.

Out went Florrie, who retired aged 76, closely followed by her fawning clientele, the tough Irish labourers. A few tables were overturned one lunchtime in protest at the soaring price of bitter in their newly scrubbed-up second home but the culprits were then banned for life. In their place came clusters of lawyers, office workers, newspapermen and councillors. None of them drank as much as the thirsty Irish but they paid the new prices without protest and preferred the new plush surroundings to the bar's former wild west appearance.

"This has changed," announced a shocked Frank, a devotee of the freewheeling atmosphere that existed in the old bar. "What's happened? There is no talk of treason these days and no jukebox. Not the same. Why does progress always destroy character and atmosphere? This new beer has a fancy name but is as tasteless as that cheap chandelier. I am not keen on this new suited lot either. Like the beer, they are full of gas.

"Which reminds me, Ralph. Strange things are happening in here and stranger things are happening in the union. As well as all the work and trouble associated with what's happening on the industrial front, that dreaded Quisling is back. We think someone has been spilling the beans to the police and government, as in 1972. In our eyes it's a kind of treason in our no grassing culture. Our adversaries know what's happening in our ranks even before some of our members get the news through our pit branches.

"I have been thinking for some time about what's been happening. The information, which will be used by the government to hamper the union in the event of a strike, must come from high up in our leadership. I have a funny feeling I know who it is. Couldn't believe it at first. But things are beginning to fit together like a jigsaw puzzle. I'll have more on this matter when we next meet."

They had a couple of beers, discussed the bitter conflict that was igniting the coalfields – though the strike was still months away - and then said cheerio.

It was obvious there was treachery afoot in the union, but Ralph had other things on his mind, not only with the impending strike that would almost paralyse the nation but with Joan. She had returned from America and as she was born in Northfield and had a fledging knowledge of the workings of the union was sent north by her boss to prepare for the inevitable industrial war.

"Are we going to have a pint in Florrie's bar?" she asked him on the phone, having booked in at The Queens once again. "It will be nice to see the old girl again."

"Sorry, love, that old bar has disappeared in the name of progress. It's full of lawyers at lunch times and early evenings. Your merry old mates, the drunks, have decamped to the pub down the road. On one of the walls in the new bar there is a large mural of a penny farthing being ridden by a little man in Victorian clothes and top hat. Also there are lots of colourful wallpaper and framed photographs of old street scenes in Northfield to keep him company.

"Pretty grotty, mock sophistication, I am afraid, but the customers like it. It's now called, wait for it, The Penny Farthing Bar. The barmaid serves cheese toasties at lunch times. That's real news, the kind of food unheard of in Florrie's days when you were lucky to get crisps."

Joan, unruffled by the remark that her so-called old pals were unrepentant boozers, said: "It will have to be the cocktail bar, and I'll buy. I can recall your northern thriftiness and your parsimonious wage packet. Or is the word impecunious rather than parsimonious? Remember? Long words and Don's rollockings? Use short words and shame the devil, he said.

"Not had the chance since unpacking at the hotel to have a look at the old cocktail bar. Pleasant memories, though. Those martinis were gorgeous. Better than in the West End. Never had anything like them elsewhere."

Ralph, unruffled by her recourse to lampoon the size of his salary, replied: "That's gone, no more fancy drinks served there. The cocktail bar is now a cloakroom. People in Northfield can't afford cocktails anymore and, anyway, such drinks are no longer fashionable even in the south."

Joan, now startled by the amount of change taking place in the hotel, commented: "So what's happened to your old flame, Betty?"

Ralph, now ruffled, added: "She doesn't work anymore - now lives with me. We are an item."

There was a protracted silence at the other end of the line. Then, having recovered from the initial shock, she said: "How could you, Ralph? How could you? Why have you done such a thing to me?"

It was now his turn to be embarrassingly silent for a few moments before he said: "Your last remark implies there is an element of emotion lingering there. Surely you are not bothered about our relationship. Not after that brutal termination all those years ago. Sometimes I do not understand the complexities of women."

She added: "No, no you are okay. I do not know what happened there. You took me by surprise. Quite a shock really. I should have known that it had happened, that you had got married. But there must be something still buried deep inside me, and it just came out; I am not in control of my emotions at times like this. You do not have to worry; it won't happen again. Tomorrow, I may tell you to bog off for good.

"Does the fact that you are married mean you are not coming to see me? Does that old-fashioned working-class ritual that husbands do not leave the home to meet members of the opposite sex still exist? If not, I need your help and your contacts. Northfield is now full of strange faces after all these years, and I do not recognise many of the shops.

"You know what will happen if I am left in this hotel and start thinking about my horrific incarceration all those years ago. I'll breakdown. Even this hotel is an alien place. No Florrie's bar, no cocktail bar and the bedrooms and restaurant have gone downhill once again. At least the last time it had a Polynesian-themed restaurant with an exotic menu but now it's back to grotty English food. There isn't even a car park; you must use a public car park and that's a few minutes' walk away.

"Sometimes I deal with too much change. You may not understand as you are a permanent fixture in this dump of a town. One day I am motoring around Manhattan, within a few days I am in London and then I'm exiled to the frozen north in this country. Have a heart, Ralph."

Back home he walked into the living room where Betty, whose plain and honest face displayed warm feelings and emotional pain too easily for her own good, did not realise anything was wrong.

His petite wife who had brown short curly hair and wore plain clothes had been preparing the table for tea by smoothing out the creases in the tablecloth in her own pernickety way. She did not look up and therefore did not see the hound dog expression that would have told her there had been a ruinous row at work or that Joan was back in town.

"You know, love, I have had a right day today. Did some shopping and my feet are killing me. Went to mums and she is no better. You'll have to go next door because Susan's sink is blocked and she can't cope now that she is in her 70s. Hurry up, dear, get your skates on. We haven't all day."

He never said a word.

"What is it, love?" she asked, now staring at his peeved face. "What's happened? The sack? Oh, dear, it's not Joan, is it? Can't be. I thought she was in America. Is she pumping you for information about the miners? Why doesn't she leave us alone?"

After he had explained what had happened and that Joan was a lost little girl in her hometown, Betty eventually relented against her better judgement. She said that he had to see her given that he was the only journalist in Northfield who had an idea about what was happening in the union and who understood how miners' minds worked.

"I know you once said that a Conservative government minister asked the leadership of the Trades Union Congress what made miners tick, that his party did not understand them, and the leaders of the other unions replied that they did not know them either. Miners, including their leaders, were seen as a breed apart by everyone else.

"I am telling you straight. If there is anything that starts between you and her, then I'll leave. I won't look right nor left I'll just walk out, straight down the street and that will be it. There'll be no coming back. Against my better judgement I am going to trust you this once. You are a decent man, Ralph, except when it comes to her.

"I do not understand the woman. I got on well

with her in the cocktail bar, but I was puzzled why she bolted so fast from Northfield and why she screwed you up. You were a dead loss for months. There were times when I could virtually touch your loneliness, it was that heavy. I picked you up, giving you a fresh start in life, but I won't do it again. Not likely. Women like her ought to have a public health warning strapped to their pretty faces.

"Don't think you can sneak up to her bedroom in an evening. I have friends in high places, remember, including the attic in the hotel. There's Brenda on reception who'll keep an eye on the staircase; Pamela and Jennifer the maids will know who has been sleeping in the bed and Carol and Susan serve breakfasts. Every corner has been covered. Oh, and Larry the night porter will keep an eye on the revolving door in the hotel entrance in case there is a temporary receptionist on duty.

"I know I'm no match for Joan. I show my feelings, but rarely do I talk about them – not even to you. I have put a lot into this marriage, it's cost a few bob, and I do not want it destroyed. But it's not up to me now. It's in your hands – if you can keep them off that woman."

News always travelled fast in Northfield. The next day, Don, sitting at the same newly polished desk that had propped up his elbows for 20 years, already knew she was back in town and grinned ruefully at Ralph as he walked towards his typewriter.

"I saw a friend of yours striding down Market Hill as I came to work this morning," he grinned.

"Looked in fine fettle. Always had an exemplary set of legs, a joyful sight to a man of my age. Back in town for the coalfield fireworks, is she? I bet she's ruffled a few bed sheets in London. Is she going to do the same in Northfield?

"I think she saw me but pretended to peer into shop windows as she sauntered along. She must still feel guilty about not working her notice. What do you think, Ralph?"

He looked sharply at his prize pupil, trying to ascertain from the expression whether there were any feelings for her behind that mask. Ralph stared back, hard and emotionless, and Don's eyes returned to his old typewriter and that editorial chestnut, the dreaded Onlooker column.

The other reporters, all newcomers, listened to the conversation and looked at each other in bewilderment. None of them had heard of Joan or Ralph's relationship with the femme fatale. All they knew was that he was apparently happily married to warm hearted Betty, who was much loved by them all since she often provided wonderful suppers at their modest home for late night visitors from the office.

At work his time was spent reporting on a wildcat strike at the 2,000-employee Dodworth Colliery, where a popular miner had been sacked for striking his boss. At another pit overtime had been banned by the union. Meanwhile, all the combatants were waiting impatiently for the trigger that would provoke a national strike and thereby threaten the economic stability of the nation. It would come, the pundits declared, with a closure of a coal mine but which one?

Much to Betty's displeasure he was spending more time at the hotel, exchanging reporters' notes with Joan and guiding her in the direction of the miner's wife who was already preparing the groundwork for the inevitable soup kitchens. The following day he gave her the name of a press officer employed by the NCB who would outline management's attitude to what was happening in the local coalfield.

It was a workmanlike relationship between the former lovers and above board for the time being: Betty's pals were stalking the hotel on her behalf and any shenanigans would lead to the poisoned gossip being sent down the ever-reliable grapevine. Once his wife's mind was made up to leave him she would be vindictive.

The powder-kegs in the coalfield and in his marriage exploded one evening while he was watching the regional news on television in March 1984. The eighth item to be screened highlighted the proposed closure of the nearby Cortonwood Colliery, which employed nearly 1,000 men.

"What are they doing?" thundered Ralph, directing his vitriol at the regional television news chiefs who had failed to understand the significance of this item. It should have been the main story, he concluded – even top of the news list on the national news programme. He knew the union would not condone the closure of a mine with sizeable reserves of coal and therefore a nationwide strike ballot was on its way.

"This means the strike will go ahead," he told a grim looking Betty whose siblings were miners, and she knew what a strike would mean to them: mounting household bills, embarrassing visits to soup kitchens and violence on picket lines.

Ralph grabbed his coat from the back of a chair and headed out of the house without saying a word, leaving behind his front door key on the table and poor Betty slumped on the settee. She knew the miners were preparing for the start of a war and that her marriage, which she had cherished for seven good years, was now coming to an end. She never could compete with Joan, more attractive and more intelligent than the homely former barmaid who loved once in her life.

He was determined not to succumb to Joan's wily ways but was prepared to help with her assignment in Northfield, realising that phone numbers of key figures, background information, analysis and the handing over of his own shorthand notes written up after union meetings would lead to a flush of cheques issued in gratitude by her proprietors.

At the end of one evening they had forgotten the time. Ralph had been talking to a union official he had met by chance while Joan phoned her latest story to the newspaper in London. Afterwards they were sitting in the Queen's lounge, their latest refuge, which was less popular than The Penny Farthing bar, and therefore there were fewer interruptions from people he knew.

"What are you going to do?" Joan asked as he glanced at his watch, both realising in horror that closing time was impending. "What's Betty going to say? Looks bad when you roll in at 11.30pm without any alcohol on your breath. Do you realise we have been drinking coke all night? She'll add two and two together and think we have been in bed somewhere else rather than drinking two feet apart in a hotel. As you say in this wretched little town, I do not fancy your chances."

Without saying anything he rose from his chair, and she looked directly into his eyes: "Well, you know where to come if she kicks you out. Back here. There will be a warm welcome.

"Oh, have you the key to the office?"

"Why?" he asked, not taking any real notice.

"For a change we could try Don's ancient desk and make sweet music," she said, giggling and then laughing, having realised she had resorted to a cliché again.

"Oh, that seriously long face in the office of long ago. Don's awful mug when I had made a mistake. Make sweet music? A cliché. He would have grumbled and told me to find other words."

"Sweet music? Symphony or a short catchy number with plenty of trumpet?" Ralph replied, finally catching on.

"Up to you, darling, provided the bells chime."

"Better not; I'm going home."

He walked out of the hotel, heading down the hill with a sense of foreboding but hoping that Betty would forgive him for being so late. Everything would be okay, he concluded. On turning the corner of their street he was not so sure. The front door was locked and there was no key in his pocket. The lights were out, the house was like a mausoleum, and he wondered whether his wife was even there. Betty, however, turned over in bed and pretended not to hear the incessant hammering on the front door.

On returning to the hotel, he spoke to the young lady he knew on the night shift in reception and was soon heading up the stairs to Joan's bedroom. The grapevine would be buzzing the following morning but he did not care anymore. There was nothing else he could do, he told Don the next day, and his boss did not believe him for the first time in years.

Chapter 17

Joan stayed in town for a few weeks and Ralph never returned home, moving in with a colleague in a flat. Betty remained in their two-up-and-two down wondering what she had done in the past to warrant such a muddled life. She never gave him a second thought after the break-up, for he had self-destructed in her opinion and that was it. Meanwhile, after a few months working on non-mining projects outside the coalfields Joan returned to Northfield to pick-up where she left off.

"The strike is well under way, and I think we should go onto the moor and see what happens tonight," Ralph told Joan one afternoon in a coffee bar. "There's talk in the union that two men are going to break the strike and go back to work at Blackmoor Colliery. It's a big mine with a militant workforce. The two men will be bused through the picket line at the entrance to the pit yard, the police will be there in force and that means trouble. It will make you a good feature article. Lots of atmosphere and pyrotechnics to light up the sky at night and your front page as well."

Joan was from the other side of town where the

houses were large and the gardens and lawns even larger, and she never understood why workers went on strike; she believed in capitalism and free market forces, a younger version of Margaret Thatcher.

"I know you lurch towards the left, Ralph, but surely you can't argue that the coal mines are losing buckets of money, and that the poor old taxpayer foots the bill. Surely it makes sense to close uneconomic pits. Doesn't it?"

He replied: "Perhaps. But it's the destruction of a way of life that bothers me. Men and families will be swept away when the coalfields close and in their place will come low paid jobs and impoverishment. I went to school with the lads who are now fighting for their jobs. They do not like me. I am a Quisling in their eyes, sold my soul to the press proprietors for a few shillings and I write untruths about their cause. They are wrong of course but you can't convince them. Not at all and it's a great shame."

Carrying torches and wearing extra clothing to keep warm during the night, they teamed up with a staff photographer, Roger, who was probably the best-known man in Northfield, and a useful ally when reporters found themselves in trouble with the public. He could talk himself out of a concentration camp.

The pit was situated on the edge of moorland. Lanes criss-crossed the area, there were a few scattered farmsteads and fewer streetlights. Light-footed men who seemed to be at home in the darkness, having worked underground for decades, knew their way around the landscape even at 2am, and appeared in front of them without warning. Torchlights were flashed in the direction of their faces and the men demanded to know who the interlopers were. Upon being told they were reporters, the leader turned nasty and snapped at Ralph: "Why have you brought a woman to a place like this? It's hell."

After the union men had moved quietly into the night, she squeezed his right hand and whispered: "Why are they so old fashioned? Don't they realise women can look after themselves? Don't they realise I survived days incarcerated in a dungeon years ago? It developed my character, a formative experience, though I did not think that at the time. Today bosses curl their toes when I enter the room."

A few yards farther along the lane leading to the colliery, she paused and asked: "What's the noise over there?" With her eyes trying to probe the darkness, she added: "I cannot see a thing. What is it? You are like the miners here; your eyes seem to be designed for the night. Mine are not."

"You can't see the faces of the men," he replied, "but they have lamps and torches and are dismantling the dry-stone walls, so they'll have missiles to chuck at the police over there and stones with which to build makeshift barricades."

He pointed to a bonfire near the gates of the colliery where miners were warming their hands, chanting union slogans, and hurling insults at lines of police armed with batons and riot shields.

Then he guided her eyes to the figure of a man

peering into the night. He was standing on the doorstep of his farmstead, the front door was open, and he was bathed in light from the kitchen. The rest of the dwelling was in darkness – the family were presumably asleep – and the peaceful scene seemed incongruous at a time when hell was breaking out all around. The farmer did not say a word, did not try to intervene but was listening to the ominous noise of one of his well-maintained walls being pulled apart for unlawful purposes.

It was soon time for the NCB minibus to appear. In the distance to their left, for a moment, two headlamps pierced the sky like searchlights as the vehicle came over the rise of the hill. Then the beams refocused on the road ahead, after which the driver stepped on the accelerator on his way to the pit's main entrance. The trio were standing on what was supposed to be a pavement as the minibus sped past and for the first time in his life Ralph saw in the improving light of the approaching dawn the fear frozen on the faces of the two passengers.

"Did you see that?" he told Joan. "Those two are either the bravest men in England or the most foolish. You could see terror in their eyes.

"They must be desperate and short of money. When this is all over, they won't be able to walk down the street without being ostracized by the men who did not return to work until the union gave the go ahead."

The bus slowed down to a few mph on approaching the gates, resulting in bottles and stones being thrown by a huddled group of pickets who also kicked and hammered the sides and reinforced windows of the vehicle with their fists. While policeman pushed, punched and cleared away the rioting miners and official picket line at the main gate, the driver drove into the relative safety of the pit yard. The driver and passengers alighted, swearing and sweating, and the high, heavy metal gates behind them were shut and another perilous journey was over. Fighting continued in the road outside the colliery for 15 minutes and arrests were made, the ringleaders being frogmarched away by the police, and the injured on both sides were given medical treatment.

Ralph, who was standing 200 yards from the hostilities, remained silent during the exchanges and after the brimstone in the air cleared he returned to the spot where she was waiting some distance away. She said something which he did not hear. He vowed not to return the following night since the angry scenes were so disturbing. He had seen one former school pal, once a law-abiding man, split open the face of a policemen by using a wooden shaft. The hatred sparking from his pal's eyes in the confrontation remained etched in his nightmares for years.

"Where's Roger?" asked Joan, worried about the fate of the photographer who had crept within yards of the warring factions to take photographs.

"Don't worry about him," Ralph replied, smiling. "That's why we brought him. All the miners know who he is and by now he'll be talking and laughing about football with his bruised pals over there. He's more to worry about from an irrational cop who'll want to get his own back on the pickets by clobbering an easy target in the shadows when no-one is looking."

"Why is Roger so popular?" Joan asked.

"That's easy. When Roger turns up at the Northfield football ground on match days, the kop is usually full and the spectators shout, applaud and urge him to give them a wave as he settles down to take photographs of the action from a spot behind the goals. He obliges and joins in the fun. They love him. It's part of the camaraderie of football. Had I gone into that picket line, they would have given me a good clobbering, for it's easy to inflict violence on a lone reporter who has no allegiance to anyone. Miners do not like writers."

All three walked back to Joan's parked car in silence. The bonfire was still burning, the hardcore of pickets reassembled near the pit gates while their mates went home to catch-up on sleep and one detachment of policemen was replaced by another. The strike-breakers did not venture underground to work since there were not enough of them to operate the colliery and therefore remained in the offices until the end of their allotted shift. Then the minibus returned them to safe houses but not before having to brave another barrage of insults and missiles, now a daily ritual.

Back at the hotel Joan was lying naked on the

bed, manipulative and alluring as ever, and she tantalised him as his eyes roamed her still shapely body, lingering on her breasts and then moving downwards to feast elsewhere.

She startled him by exclaiming in jest: "Do not be so rude. You are staring. Can't a girl have any privacy?" She was smiling wantonly and, ignoring her comments, he walked over and kissed her full on the lips before both slipped between the sheets for the rest of the night.

The next morning he revealed the news that had been kept secret for years; he wasn't sure how she would take it – would she burst into tears or instead threaten to tear down the town in one cataclysmic demolition job to find her kidnapper?

"What's up, darling?" she asked, now in a suspicious mood that soon turned vindictive. "That furrowed brow is not becoming. What's troubling you – not those silly miners again? It will be over soon, and you'll be able to return to your idyllic life at the Advertiser. Don and you. What a couple. An old boring man and another who has deserted his poor wife, left her in the lurch like an old-fashioned cad. What a combination to have in the same office."

She laughed out loud, first mockingly and then accusingly, and she gave a perfect rendition of Don addressing the office during one of his pep talks, complete with errs, pregnant pauses and the occasional dropped aitch. He had forgotten her skills at mimicry, which made her sound so cheap.

The sniggering soon stopped.

"I think I know who the man with the cast in the eye is."

She frowned and climbed quickly out of bed, reaching for her dressing gown to cover her nakedness.

"I do not know what you mean. Are you talking about that monster down in the cellar? How do you know? Who is it? Come on I want to know. No use saying something like that then withholding the rest of the information. You beast."

It was his turn to tantalise as she glared at him.

"I am not sure whether I should," he added, giving her a fake mean look and at the same time trying to remove her dressing gown which she hugged around her body like a comfort blanket, as if reliving in her mind something ugly from long ago in the cellar.

"Get away," she demanded angrily. "Do not touch me. Come on, who was it? Do you know him?"

Ralph wasn't taking it that seriously, first poking gentle fun at her distressed condition in retaliation at her comment about leaving Betty in the lurch and then trying in a sado-masochistic manoeuvre to make love to her while she was mentally vulnerable.

His robust advances were resisted in a vicious outburst. Blood was drawn when she bit deeply into his right arm and at the same time she let out a savage cry as she beat his chest with fists. He never said a word and stood there taking the punishment for several minutes until, exhausted and defeated, she slumped into a chair. He never said a word and walked out of the room.

"Okay," she said, a few hours later. She was smoking a cigarette for the first time in years and was fully dressed, sitting at a table in The Penny Farthing bar. "You know what I want."

"The name is Pinder. He's an old man but I have no idea where he lives.

"Is he related to Mark, the MP?" she asked, surprised.

"Yes; Mark's his nephew but I have no idea of an address. It appears he went off to live in Spain on your father's money, disappeared for years. Now back in town."

"How do we find him?"

"Not sure," replied Ralph. Then he laughed and said Peter would come to the rescue.

"Who? Not the cheeky Co-op delivery lad who was the housewives' favourite, delivering groceries along with sexual prowess? What a man! Is he still alive?"

"I think so. A tough miner found him in bed with the wife and that was it. Peter nearly ended up a physical wreck after the fisticuffs, but Peter Pan was taught a lesson and abandoned the bike. He is now manager of a small supermarket in Northfield. What's more important he still knows where everyone lives. It's a kind of hobby of his. Perhaps he's gone back into business with the ladies. Who knows?"

Joan rather than Ralph went to see him at his shop, and she never revealed a word about what she learned, but Peter, the Jack-the -lad, continued to fascinate her.

"You know, Ralph, he's changed," she said, smiling. "I can remember the Tony Curtis haircut, The Beatle hair style and the short back and sides when he was a Mod.

"Have you seen him recently?"

"No."

"Well, he is still smart and sharp with the retort but he's bald. Bald as a badger...."

Ralph gave her a phoney dirty look as he was up to mischief again: "Spoiler warning. Bald as a badger is a cliché. A bad one.."

She nearly lost her temper: "You and your cliches. Is Don pulling the levers again? Your term 'spoiler warning' isn't exactly original material either, is it?"

"What did he say about Pinder?"

"Not telling. You are not being nice to me today."

He concluded: "We are heading for a row. Let's change the subject."

Like all women she tried to have the last word: "Peter is an attractive man. I have always thought that. Had I been born on a council estate I might have taken him on. A blissful thought."

Ralph's face darkened: "Do not dare."

He was worried she would do something foolish now she had the name of her tormentor, but his mind was distracted by the strike. Again, he suggested they went to view what was happening at another pit where four strike-breakers were preparing to be bused in.

This time the colliery – Redmead – was located next to a council estate and not far from the main road. Pickets carrying banners were lined up at the entrance to the narrow lane leading to the pit; the two journalists found a vantage point high on a road bridge 300 yards away from the battle lines. The pickets' hut, a makeshift structure made from old doors and broken wooden fences, and where all the men met during the day, was also in view. It was known as The Alamo.

"Whereabouts are we?" Her local geography had been flimsy even while working in Northfield and she added: "The news desk may want some colour in my piece and that may require descriptive details about this and neighbouring localities."

Having answered her questions without suspecting anything, he continued to peer at what was going off as he listened to hooves resounding on the pit lane: a mounted police squad was quartered in the pit yard after tensions rose earlier in the dispute. Now the riders were preparing to take up positions to keep the pickets away from the police convoy that would escort the NCB minibus carrying the black legs into the pit yard.

It was 6am, time for the convoy to arrive. The miners and police were gearing up for a fight and an empty almost derelict shop 100 yards away from the picket lines burst into flames. It was the work of a small group of wild pickets or local troublemakers who without any associations with mining had joined in the fun. He turned to face her and pointed out that one of the retained firemen who manned the approaching fire engine was one of his friends, a miner. That man had a conflict of loyalties - he would have the unenviable task of fighting the flames with full-time firemen as well facing simultaneously the wrath of the firebrands with whom he worked underground.

He could be beaten up by his mates, Ralph told his surprised girlfriend. With miners you were either with them or against them, he added. The following day the part-time firefighter would remove his uniform and then line up on the picket line with his striking work mates again - facing the anger of the police phalanx. Within a couple of days he would be back with the firefighters for another shift and the cycle of conflict would start again.

A few minutes later Ralph turned to explain another situation to Joan, but she had left his side. He looked around in the inadequate morning light; he shivered in the wind and peered towards the horizon but there was no sign.

At that time he wasn't unduly worried as she may have had to find a toilet at one of the nearby houses where lights were shining in the kitchens. He later became more concerned as the noise generated by the warring factions reached a crescendo. The convoy was approaching the pit, and a disturbing thought took hold that she may have wandered into the war zone to get a better picture of what was happening.

"Where is she?" he thought. "God, what's happened?"

He turned his back on the battlefield, now illuminated by the flames shooting through the roof of the old shop. As the air filled with smoke and the wailing of police sirens he headed to the spot where her car was parked. That had gone as well.

Chapter 18

Joan was looking forward to her target for that night. She had not said anything to Ralph but on being told the names of the districts near the Redmead Colliery she realized that Pinder, her arch enemy, lived in one of the nearby streets. What luck. What fun.

While Ralph was witnessing the drama on the picket line, Joan was walking down the footpath leading to a council bungalow on a strangely quiet estate, only a few minutes' stroll from the battlefield. She was thankful that Peter, the supermarket manager, had a photographic memory and knew where the old monster lived.

It took several minutes of intense knocking on the front door to elicit an "Who is it?" from the occupant. There was another "Who is it?", this time louder and more anxious than the first, and she smiled and rubbed her woollen gloves in glee. She remained cool, though, and that steel-bar in her character that had helped her to survive the ordeal in the underground prison reasserted itself. She was soon relishing the thought of meeting him face-to-face without his balaclava

"I'm from the police," she announced in a bossy voice. "Nothing to worry about, Mr Pinder. We want a word. We are worried that several of the pickets have been running wild on the estate and a couple of windows have been smashed. Please open up."

There was the jangling of keys, the light in the hallway was switched on and the old man cursed under his breath as he peered short-sightedly through the pane of glass in the door.

"Just a minute, "he said. "I'll open the door, but this is a fine time to be disturbing an old man. What do you want?"

The door was opened, and Joan pushed her way into the bungalow, suddenly realising that he was in a wheelchair. She quickly shut the front door, after which she grabbed the rear of the wheelchair and hauled its protesting occupant into the living room.

"What are you doing?" he shouted in alarm, struggling to rise but falling back defeated onto the seat. "You are not the police; what do you want?"

He threw a punch, a feeble effort from an old man, and Joan was waiting for an excuse to give him a good hiding despite his age. She slapped him unmercifully across the face, one of her Stuka dive-bombers that had put Ralph in his place and enjoyed every second of it.

"Well, do you recognise me?" asked Joan, grinding her teeth in anticipation of what was coming. "Come on, who am I?"

He was slobbering, a pitiful shadow of the thug who had bullied her all those years ago:

"No, I don't. I am going to shout my head off and my next-door neighbour will hear. He'll come to the rescue."

Prepared for that contingency, she removed from her handbag a nylon stocking that was stuffed into his mouth, as his pal had done in the car that had whisked her away from the centre of Northfield. Then she used one of Ralph's old ties to keep the gag in position, after which she removed two scarves from her bag and secured his arms to the wheelchair.

Her victim was too old to retaliate, and she was stronger than she thought. He cringed in the wheelchair but that made no difference as she was on a roll.

"Perhaps, old man, I should give you a few clues to refresh your senile mind. Do you remember a cellar, perhaps under a farmhouse? A long time ago. Have you heard of Two Trees you wretched old man? Well, I am going to give you a few lessons. Within a couple of minutes you'll be back in that cellar, recalling all those dreadful deeds you and your pals did but this time the boot will be on the other foot. It won't be pleasant this time around.

"Who are you?" he asked, weakly, though Joan realised he would not look her in the eyes, and she concluded that meant he remembered her imprisonment. It never occurred that she could have the wrong man. The evidence leading to her arrival at the bungalow was not copper-bottomed by any means, but she knew her instincts were right.

Peering at his creased trousers, she said: "I want

to see what you have got. Remember, you old bastard? Remember the fear that shook my body that day? Do you recall the dirty jokes you and your mates said when you saw me half undressed? Come on, they are coming off."

His spirit began to fight back. "We didn't do anything else, though, did we?" he squirmed." It could have been a lot worse. Come on, admit it. I do not deserve this."

"Oh, yes, you do," she replied, pushing him back into his wheelchair as he tried to gather the strength to fight back. She punched and slapped him. Again and again.

"The only reason why you did not do anything is that you wanted to hand me back to my father untouched to get your hands on the money. I sometimes had nightmares on that old bed in the cellar wondering what you and the rest of them were thinking about, what you were up to. I expected to be raped every night, abused and handled like a piece of meat."

He uttered: "Haven't you any mercy? It was a long time ago and you do not realise what I went through afterwards. We did feel guilty in Spain. It did trouble me. A lot. But you won't believe that, will you? You are too far gone with hate."

Without any hesitation she unbuttoned his trousers and pulled them down to his ankles, all the time giggling like a schoolgirl, and by now the man was convinced he was dealing with a psychopath, the female version, and tried to struggle free. His mind, gyrating wildly, was full of thoughts of what might happen next.

"Oh, old man, you have peed yourself, how terrible," she declared, peering at his lower regions, and laughed coarsely in his face. She walked into the kitchen and returned with a carving knife, the sight of which made him shake uncontrollably before bursting into tears.

It was at that moment she relented. She was exhausted. All the bullying and all the threats had taken it out of her, and she collapsed on the floor, relieved and happy, having avenged the treatment of her former self, the young reporter with bright eyes and a brighter future. That ordeal underground had ruined her personal life.

Bent double and slumped in the wheelchair, he continued to whine, not realising that her behaviour was now calming down and that his nightmare was coming to an end.

On impulse she decided to find if there was any incriminating evidence in his desk and cupboards, a forlorn hope after all these years but she wanted to see what motivated this man who had once terrorised families. Perhaps there was a prized possession, a relic from the age of black markets. The family's photographic album, the first item to catch her attention, was full of young and smiling faces and groups of adults sitting in deckchairs on the beach at Blackpool, with the tower in the background.

On one fading photograph the men had rolled up trouser legs, casual white shirts unbuttoned at the top and prominent sets of braces; their wives wore flowery dresses, cheap sunglasses and unfashionable white sandals.

The deckchairs were defended by several turreted sandcastles in various stages of construction and topped with paper flags representing various countries, the largest being the union flag. Colourful buckets and spades had been hastily discarded on the sand by the children as they were marshalled by parents in preparation for the traditional group picture at the seaside.

An idyllic scene, it appeared on the surface. The family looked like any other enjoying themselves on the annual holidays at the seaside in the 1950s, but several of the men must have been associated with the activities of black-market gangs during the war.

For a moment she was taken in by this sentimental scene, then realised that even the commandants of German concentration camps had children who doted on their fathers. The album was thrust aside together with an old wedding album and lots of snapshots of children smiling in back yards and on recreation grounds in the 1950s and 1960s.

There were a couple of photographs she missed. One was at the bottom of the drawer: A boy aged about 11 was in football shorts and shirt and held an old-fashioned T-panelled leather football. He was grinning at the cameraman, a member of the newspaper staff. It was young Mark Pinder, so proud that he had scored four goals in a local schools' cup final, the only genuine golden moment in his life.

"I have never had the same kind of thrill that came with that football match and the medal, not even when politicians praised my speeches or presented me with awards in later life," he once told Ralph.

A second photograph revealed another aspect of his life. Holding aloft a large silver trophy, he was pictured in trunks at the local public baths, having won a series of major races in a schools' gala.

Both photographs would have earned Joan a generous bonus had she spotted them because that kind of background material was much in demand by the media when Mark later became notorious for a few weeks. (When Mary Elliott was found guilty at the Assizes in 1944, a reporter found a photograph of her in a drawer in the newspaper's photographic darkroom and made a small fortune from Fleet Street.)

The big surprise leading to the impending Pinder scandal was in a small drawer in the desk. It was a sheet of neatly folded paper. Nothing unusual about that but the words shocked her. With her mind performing somersaults, she abandoned the old man who was now so traumatised he was hallucinating and calling for his long dead wife.

Joan had one last burst of malignancy to inflict on him. Nice comforting words were whispered in his ear, making him relax a little, after which she turned nasty again, threatening to kill him if he uttered one word.

"Do me a favour, Pinder," she said before making her way to the front door. "Just die and leave everyone in peace."

Refreshed and relishing the rich praise heaped on her by the bosses in London, having submitted a series of perceptive articles on the strike, she joined Ralph two days' later in The Penny Farthing.

"Where did you get to the other night," he asked, peering intently at her, hoping her eyes would reveal a clue but as usual the look she returned was unfathomable.

"Here and there, you know," came the anaemic reply. "Perhaps I found a robust boyfriend among the lads from the Met."

"Do not mention those policemen," he replied. "I had a nasty brush with them a couple of weeks ago and later found an injured miner in a country lane with 'You Have Met the Met' sticker on his clothes. I even understand the local police are investigating the theft of a television from a community hall where they have been billeted."

Her pensive little girl lost look meant more bad news was on its way and his guts were prepared for the inevitable ... "I am sorry Ralph but ..."

"I'm leaving later today," she said, her eyes downcast. "I am being called back to the London office. They have been pleased with my material, but they want a new pair of eyes to look at the strike. I have enjoyed it here as usual, but I am worried about you.

"Why don't you give up that silly job of yours and divorce Don in the office? Come back to London with me. You'll get work and if you don't my salary is good enough for both of us. There's still my inheritance. Once poor old dad dies in Spain I'll be loaded. It would not be a bad life for both of us. I have got on better with you than anyone else. Think about it."

There was no reaction from Ralph, for he gave her one of his infamous blank looks and she changed course: "You are not thinking of going back to Betty, are you? Nice, dependable old Betty, the barmaid. Ralph, you need motivating and getting out of the Northfield bubble with all its constraints, busy bodies and attitudes that belong to the year dot."

Her face darkened: "You do not change, do you? You rarely said that you loved me in our early days, these days you are entirely mute on the matter. Three simple words. 'I love you'. They come too easily to some men but not you.

"Padlocked away in your own dreamy world, aren't they? Never to be heard in daylight. Always hidden away, as if they are dirty.

"Why do I bother? Come on, speak up. Now's your chance. Endorse our love. Finally say something. I know how you feel but I need to be told. Every woman wants to hear those words. I have feelings, you know, and needs.

"Can you recall what Don said? Ask her for a date and you'll have lunch at the Dorchester in London. I think he even said that I would blow you out in bubbles. What cheek!!"

Avoiding the questions, Ralph said: "It's no use, Joan. This time I'm prepared for the break. I won't get churned up; I realise you'll always want to be on the move. I enjoy your company but the physical side this time around got a bit out-of-hand, and I found myself in a kind of no man's land. Blame my puritanical upbringing for the guilt but that's it. I am staying here.

"I will be around for your next visit. Full stop. You'll be back again and perhaps we'll celebrate on the old office desk."

Looking at his watch, he realised the first editions of the evenings were arriving in Northfield and that a feature written by his former colleague, Phil, would provide a new slant on the strike.

A few minutes later he returned to the bar, having bought a copy from Sammy, the newspaper seller whose patch was outside the entrance to the bus station.

"Do you remember Phil?" he asked as he sat down and glanced at the main story on the front page. "You remember he did some good stories for the Advertiser."

The lead story was not about the strike but had been written by Phil, now based at the Northfield branch office. Trawling down the column to see whether it would be of interest to Advertiser readers, Ralph's eyes stumbled upon the name Pinder. He glanced at Joan who realised at once what was in the newspaper and she turned away from his gaze to buy another drink.

"Have you seen this?" he asked grimly, his anger starting to inflate. "You went to see Pinder the other night while we were supposed to be keeping an eye on the picket line. You callous, devious cow. How could you do this?"

"What?" she replied, acting surprised. "What's happened? Something nasty I hope."

The story stated an elderly man was beaten up in his own home and had been found terrified and injured by neighbours the following morning. The householder, named locally as Michael Pinder, had been left so traumatised he was unable to be interviewed by police officers.

"This is the good bit," Ralph added with a weak smile. "The police suspect teenagers conned their way into the bungalow and beat him up. There is even an editorial in the newspaper saying it was time police cracked down on teenage violence and that corporal punishment ought to be resurrected as a deterrent.

"You are the one who did this. Teenagers my foot. The perpetrator was a brutal middle-aged woman who wanted to kick the guts out of an old man. Do you know this could get me into trouble? I should go to the police and tell them what really happened."

"You won't – you have too much allegiance to me. Fathead. I needed to do it. You did not suffer while I was held captive in that dreadful cellar. That man nearly destroyed my life. I'll never regret what I have done. He had it coming. What's more I enjoyed kicking him; I am fed up with being a lady. I kicked over the traces."

Ralph: "That's taken me back with a bang. Old Mary Elliott said she wanted to kick over the traces and that's why she nearly bankrupted a coal mine to give herself a lifestyle that almost belonged to royalty.

"I sometimes do not understand you or Mary Elliott. Both of you are alike in many respects. You each lead contradictory lives. On the surface you are successful, but it's come at a price, as with Mary.

"You have a brilliant career, for instance. But what do you do with your new pals in London - bedroom gymnastics in a swanky hotel? Bed hopping from one newspaper to another?"

"I never do anything of the sort, "she replied, annoyed. "So that is what you think. Jealously on your part? I suspect you went through hell for a time after our break-up, believing that I had turned into a classy prostitute. Yes, I bet you did. You were all screwed-up at that time and your emotions went through purgatory. Sorry to disappoint you. In London I worked most of the time, hard and relentless shifts, and I had the occasional spot of fun."

She gave him a quizzical look which slowly turned warm hearted once her intuition indicated that the police would not be tipped off.

"Keep it to yourself, Ralph. Let the police do the work. Pinder won't say anything when he comes around since he's done enough in his grubby life to be fed to the sharks. If you keep your deliciously sweet lips tightly closed on this issue, I'll give you something for your trouble. Never mind, I'll give it to you anyway."

Chapter 19

Withdrawing from her handbag the sheet of paper discovered in the drawer at Pinder's home, she gave him a lesson in verbal abuse, for she was still recovering from his accusations that she led a low life in London.

"Instead of reading your pal's words in that rag, why don't you scan that list of names? Jaw-dropping, isn't it? Perhaps you do not know but I have checked several of those phone numbers with head office: they are contact numbers for Special Branch. One of our journalists is well in with them.

"Now I do not want to write a story about Pinder's nephew, your beloved MP, contacting our secret service about what's happening in the miners' union and divulging all their strike plans. My Editor will believe that your MP is doing a fine patriotic job by helping to destroy the left-wing cancer that's eating away at our beautiful democratic system. I know your loyalties exist elsewhere and you'll want to follow this one up. So that's my leaving present.

"I am not sure how you are going to square the fact that your old pal, the shooting star in the Labour Party, is, in fact, a fifth columnist. Have you got the guts to go through with this one? It will be very interesting, and I'll watch carefully from a fancy bar in the West End. Perhaps even have a cocktail for a change and wish you well.

"On that note I'll leave you, darling, and I'll see you next time I'm in town. Meanwhile, get divorced from Don. I still love you, have always done so since the days when we rattled out stories on those old typewriters, but I am waiting for you to grow up and get away from the old man.

"I have forgotten one thing. The last time you were in trouble with the police, when I was released from that dungeon, what did they say? You perverted the course of justice by withholding vital evidence."

He replied grudgingly: "Trust you to say you love me then drop a bombshell from the past. Nothing much happened. Don intervened, had a word with his police cronies and smoothed things out as usual. Detectives had to charge me, but they put in a good word with the prosecution service and the magistrates, all romantics who were convinced I did it for love. I was given a suspended sentence. My young age was taken into consideration as well.

"This time the situation has changed; I'll be on my way to jail if they find out I know who beat-up Pinder."

The prospect of another face-to-face encounter with the police did not bother him. It was the fact that she had left him defeated again that was worrying. After her first departure his emotions were mangled; this time his principles were being questioned when it came to a close friend, Mark, leaving him screwed up.

How could he publicly crucify a pal without squashing his own conscience? Surely the office guru knew.

His meeting with Don was delayed, however, for the inevitable had happened. The crusty veteran had finally reached retirement age – 65 – and in his honour a party was held in the office one evening. Not that he would disappear off the scene as he planned to continue working part-time as a proofreader, correcting reporters' copy and acting as a kind of consultant on the town of Northfield since the year AD 84.

The staff organised a buffet, free drinks and a mock Mastermind quiz, with everyone joining in the fun. Despite their cutting remarks behind his back, most of the staff and many ex-reporters respected him.

Several successful newspaper executives who had started at the Advertiser returned to Northfield to join in the celebrations, having realised late in their careers that managing a swarm of lively and intelligent young journalists was the most difficult job in the industry.

"What did Mark Twain say about his father?" one of executives asked his pal. "As a young man I thought he was the most stupid person I had ever known but a few years later I thought he wasn't so bad?"

The other man said: "Something like that. As

angry young men we must have helped Don to become the grumpy man of today. We were stroppy and challenged his decisions in the office. How did he manage to run a newspaper full of young misfits in those days?"

His companion: "It wasn't all one-way traffic. I have the imprint of his boots on my emotions. It took weeks of mental pummelling from him to teach me where to place apostrophes. It was torture."

Rather than concentrate on serious topics as in the celebrated television programme, the office chose the light-hearted subject, The Life and Times of Don (1866-1980).

To give the scene authenticity, the office lighting was switched off and the unfortunate contestant was required to squint into a low-powered photographer's studio spotlight as he sat behind his desk. The programme's sombre background sound effects were ineptly re-created by volunteers, thereby creating more laughter among the 20-strong audience, which included reporters, sub editors, photographers and guests from other departments.

"Question one: Who was the mayor in 1956?" asked Baz, a reporter, who wore an evening suit, white shirt and bow tie for the event, and who had a passing resemblance to Hughie Green, a tv quizmaster. Baz was the host for the evening.

"Ald Arthur Butler," Don trumpeted, enjoying the merriment for once. Everyone knew the answer was correct as he had been on first name terms with 21 of the previous 25 mayors. "Name the mayor who died in office in 1966?" He appeared puzzled for effect then announced: "Mrs Brenda Smith."

"What was the average weekly circulation of the Advertiser in January 1958?"

"Thirty-six thousand."

The onlookers were not sure about that answer, but the consensus was that he was correct again. Did it matter whether it was right or wrong?

"What was the average circulation in August 1959?"

"The newspaper was not published that month because the printers were on strike."

"How did he remember that?" Ralph muttered to a colleague. "I did not even know there had been a strike."

"Where is Brunswick Street in Northfield?"

"Drive down Foster Street, take the third turning on the right and turn left. Ald Fred Lunn lived at No. 46."

Ralph grinned and said quietly to his mate: "I thought it was No 40 but whom am I to contradict the expert. When Don was a cub reporter he spent years tramping the streets in Northfield. Weddings and obituaries were his speciality at the age of 18. He knew everyone.

"Once he spotted the council had put a street in the wrong place on a map in the town's guidebook and caused a rumpus at the town hall. Then the council omitted the village of Jump (population 3,000) off another map. Guess what his headline was?

"'Jump jumps off the map'."

"How did you know that?" asked Ralph.

"I have a long memory like Don."

There was applause as the Memory Man rose majestically from his chair, having answered all the questions correctly. Placing hands on the desk that had seen two world wars and much amorous action from various randy reporters, he smiled in appreciation, then stepped aside and bowed like a member of the Playgoers' group at the end of a worthy performance at the theatre.

The Editor, as hard as Shap Granite when it came to work, had the glimmer of a sentimental tear in his eyes as he hailed him as the Mastermind of Northfield, handing over a cut-glass engraved bowl similar in shape but cheaper than the one awarded to the winners on television.

Ralph turned again to his colleague: "It's all very sad in a way. All that time and energy expended in acquiring what is basically useless information. What will it all mean in ten years? Nothing at all. I do not want to end like him in another 20 years, spouting local facts and recalling ancient events and having people laughing behind my back.

"Who wants to know who lived at 46, Brunswick Street, Northfield, in 1961?"

Three days later Ralph tracked him down to his new office, a virtual cubby-hole situated behind the sub editors' room. The old journalist preferred the larger office with its bonhomie and the vitality of young people, but times changed, and he had a new destiny – in the smallest office in the old building.

The Editor, who demonstrated a smidgeon of sentimentality at the retirement party, soon resorted to his old ways. He wanted Don out of the way as he saw a human fossil who could contaminate the whizzkids with his old theories and redundant work practices.

Ralph was surprised when they met: "Don? What's happened to you? You look healthy and there is a sweet smell in this place. What is it?"

"Stopped smoking and never felt better. I was going through two packets of Benson and Hedges per day and developed a funny cough. You lot won't need to have your little competitions anymore to see how long the ash remains at the end of my cig. You did not know that I knew about your little capers, did you? Thought you were having a laugh behind my back. Knew all the time. You and that crafty Phil in the old days, what a pair of cards. I called you the hippies even though you did not dress like them. Did you both take dope? You all did that in the 60s, didn't you? Now you can tell me the truth."

"No. Never."

As usual Don was not finished with the past.

"I also know what my desk was used for after the lights were switched off in an evening. I wasn't daft, you know. Phil, that over sexed pursuer of married women, wasn't the first. Where do you think I learnt about love? On my desk when I was a cub reporter. You missed out because your la-de-dah girl friend had a flat."

He changed the subject, having revealed too

much – he was worried some of his comments would reach the directors or his wife – and instead peered blankly at the wall in that windowless room. For the first time in years he concentrated on the future.

"Change is coming in for the kill for people like us. Computers will take the place of typewriters; scores of jobs will go in the printing works, and I am not sure whether newspapers will be able to survive the other innovations that will come with new forms of communication. The doom and gloom are 20 or 30 years away, but this newspaper will end up on the scrapheap like a clapped out printing press. It won't be anyone's fault. It's what is known as progress."

Laughing, he added: "I am not even sure what will happen to my old desk. I think an antique dealer is interested in buying it. What will the young 'uns do when it's moved out? I can't imagine the office without it - it's an institution. One Editor thought it must cover a big hole in the wooden floor that no-one has seen since the company took over the building in the 1920s."

"What can I do for you?" he added, changing the subject again. "Oh, how is that classy bird of yours. Run off again? Do not worry she'll be back, bad penny and all that. Nice pair of pegs. And nice…"

With a death-ray look Ralph stopped him in his tracks. After a pause Ralph said he did not know what to do about Mark Pinder, the tarnished former talisman. In his view Pinder would become dangerously discredited if all was made public.

"I could ruin his career," Ralph confessed. "In a

way that's not fair. It was my publicity that helped get him elected and he reciprocated with generous news tip-offs. I am now on the point of destroying the lot. It's an act of betrayal on my part. Treachery, in fact. Sometimes this job makes me sick."

Don: "I thought you believed in justice. What he's done is wrong, surely. It's Mark who has betrayed his colleagues, friends. I know I am not ultra white. I have known many important people in the community and sometimes I have turned a blind eye to their indiscretions but none of them matched Mark's odious record.

"At the same time he is an astute politician. I do not think he'll be easy to knobble. It could all blow back in your face. There is such a thing as libel and if there was a legal battle you would have to prove he had been leaking confidential information. That would be impossible unless you have solid incriminating evidence.

"He even brought a tear to my eyes once upon a time. I heard him speaking to hundreds of miners at a gala in Northfield. Talked about the old days, the poverty and the camaraderie. Wonderful stuff. He was silver-tongued, a dreamer and a firebrand. He mesmerized the lot of them."

Don hesitated, peering anxiously at his friend.

"Remind you of anyone?"

"Mary Elliott?"

"I was thinking of someone else."

Believing it was a joke, Ralph asked: "What about Peter the Co-op delivery boy?"

"Do not be silly. I was thinking of Joan. She's launched a campaign in her newspaper and it's highly successful. It's in a good cause but she's also adept at manipulating the readership. She's a fabulous wordsmith. Would not like the thought of her getting into the wrong hands. Political-wise, that is.

"On a personal level, she keeps coming back from the past and you take her back. She's manipulating you as well. Perhaps even laughing at you behind your back. Time to wake up, perhaps."

Once again he hesitated: "Sometimes I think you should have remained with Betty. Unattractive, solid and reassuringly predictable."

"Meanwhile, on the other subject, my advice: go and get him. He's dishonest."

As the troubled reporter walked out of the office his former boss said: "Remember the day when you were aged 19 and wanted to find the killer of Bobby Lee? You started working too hard and let yourself go. You had to take time off work. Well, you were too young then for that kind of job. You are now ready. Good luck. Perhaps you will get your name in the newspapers. Or worse - appear on ghastly television."

Chapter 20

There was no time to mess around and the MP was contacted at home at the weekend. Nothing unusual about that since they had been doing it for years, swapping news and tittle tattle and as a result a formidable working relationship was built-up.

"I need to talk," said Ralph, trying to suppress his nerves and at the same time recalling Joan's remarks that Don thought too much about the reputations of pals to be a reputable journalist.

"What's it about? Anything interesting," came the reply. "I have got something that may make you a sizeable story next week."

"No; it's serious. It's about you and what you have been doing during the miners' strike. Let your old mates down, haven't you?"

"What are you getting at? I haven't let anyone down. I have been on the picket line with the lads, given part of my salary to the strike fund and I have made speeches all over the country in support of the union. What's got into you? You have changed in the space of a week."

"It's about a list of policemen and secret service men and their phone numbers."

"You had better come to see me, and we'll sort this out."

"Where do I come?" Ralph sneered. "Two Trees on the hill, the former home of a jail bird, or to your second home at the coast. It's not fair, is it? You are living a privileged life while your old mates live on the bread line in their council houses. The real bread line, at that. One of them said he had resorted to walking into the bakers to smell the aroma of baking bread even though he couldn't afford to buy it. Life has got that bad for them."

"Don't be daft, Ralph. This is silly. You know where I live."

It was raining and dark, a mucky night in the local parlance. Two Trees had not changed that much over the years, and he thought that it seemed ironic that his pal had ended up in the gloomy house where Miss Elliott, middle class and seemingly respectable, had prepared plans to hoodwink the wealthy pit owners.

Years' later Mark, champion of the miners and as dubiously respectable as the old owner, had been equally energetic in bamboozling the union leaders. The house seemed to attract owners who ratted on their own people, Ralph concluded.

Mary had conned the pit owners and most of her village but was known as Lady Bountiful. The scout hut she had financed was a spacious, well-constructed building which put all the nearby shops and houses to shame. Mark had been a fly boy who had taken his colleagues for a bumpy ride but was also known for his love of good causes.

The lights were on in the kitchen and living room; the other rooms and bedrooms were in darkness. The MP opened the front door and there was a crystal tumbler of whiskey in his hand. Ralph decided the tumbler was a sign that he had won the first round since his pal hit the booze only when worried.

In the living room Ralph declined a drink and both sat in easy chairs facing each other while they went through the necessary preliminaries; then Ralph said: "I have a list of incriminating names and phone numbers. What do you have to say about that?"

"Look, Ralph, where did you get this fake list from? You know I wouldn't do anything to undermine or threaten the cause. You believe that don't you? I was a miner long ago; you came to see me when young and as green as they come. I helped you along the way and you did the same for me. Like brothers. Where did the alleged list come from?

"From your wretched uncle's desk. You kept it there for safety because you thought one of your pals or perhaps the cleaner would find it in your own house or office and pass it onto the union. So, what have you to say?

Mark's temper exploded: "How did you get that list? Wait a minute ...it's got nothing to do with that break-in at my uncle's bungalow? Did you give him a good going over? That was brutal. An attack on an old man - shame on you."

Ralph: "I have my own methods, and I am not

telling where the list came from. On the night of the attack I was on the picket line and there are plenty of witnesses.

"Do not change the subject. My mind has been working overtime; it's starting to come up with sensational stuff, even about Frank, the good union man.

"In the early 70s he was always going on about a mole in the union who was leaking confidential stuff to the police. Years later he was convinced that he had the right man and promised to pass the name on.

"He never did. At the beginning of the latest strike he started again, cursing the so-called traitor and then shut up. It happened so quickly. We still met in the bar where he handed over a lot of non-confidential information; I was grateful, but he never mentioned the guilty man. He never referred to anymore leaks. Perhaps the leaks dried up, but I do not think so. Strange.

"Later I spotted him driving a spanking new car. Never seen him drive before. Never talked about cars before that. Then he started showing it off to his pals. I didn't give it much thought. Now I realise you got him that car through your devious friends and that's why he was never the same with me again."

Mark remained silent. He looked flustered and did not try to deny some of the accusations. The truth was munching away inside him.

"You do not know what it's been like, Ralph. You really don't. The establishment got its knife into me years ago. Everything was fine until then. I always thought I would fail as an MP, but I didn't. I have done a decent job but in the 1972 strike I did something wrong. I got involved with a woman in London, the wife of a celebrity. She was originally from Northfield, came from a good family, and that was it.

"A few months later the men in trench coats came along and said they had photographs of us in her bedroom. Quite explicit pictures. I do not think Elaine, the woman, realised she had helped to set me up. The men were from the secret service, a special unit. We have all heard about the Russians doing that kind of thing but not our lot. They promised not to tell the Sunday newspapers provided I played ball. That's what I did. Fed them information. I have always been an honorary senior official in the miners' union; it was easy to get hold of the confidential stuff.

"When the latest strike broke out, they came to see me again. Just like blackmailers. They would not give in and always demanded their pound of flesh. I'll be in their pockets until I die. Over the last couple of years I have thought of vanishing but that's running away from a problem. No good. At first it was easy to do what they wanted, but as I have got older the old conscience has been working overtime, and I knew one day someone would coming knocking at my door. Never thought it would be you, Ralph. I thought we were pals.

"In fact, why have you suddenly become super white? I thought all newspapermen were in the pocket of their right-wing employers and that you followed the line to undermine unions. How come?"

Ralph: "During this strike I have seen things that have made me feel uneasy. It's not a case of which side is right or wrong. History moves on. But I do not like the way working class people in this town – many of whom I have known since a kid – are being mauled by life. They won't get anything out of this dispute. They'll end up licking the armpits of history. No more decent wages and instead a devastated way of life. The middle-classes with money will survive in Northfield; they always do.

"Perhaps deep down I am thinking of myself. If the economy of this town goes bust, then the local newspaper may go the same way as the pits because the advertising revenue will collapse. The National Coal Board spent a fortune advertising for miners in the good years - that's all gone."

Mark: "Surely not. I can't imagine Northfield without the Advertiser. What a thought. I have been reading the newspaper since I was a kid. I scored four goals in a junior school match, and I merited three short paragraphs of fame and a photograph. I was as proud as Punch. Top man. Thought I was Tommy Lawton. That match means more to me than anything else."

"Who?"

Mark, laughing out loud for the first time that evening, told Ralph he was not old enough to recall the legendary centre-forward.

"He had dynamite in both boots and could head a ball like John Charles, the Welsh wizard from the

1960s. You can remember him?"

Ralph, now despondent, did not answer. He looked at Mark whose eyes were glistening happily at his recollections from school days. Why did he want to crucify him in the newspaper? There was something not quite right about doing such a thing. What good would it do?

The newspaper would be blamed by the locals for ruining the career of a man who had done so much to improve life in the mining towns. Many other voters – the non-miners - would wonder what all the fuss was about, believing Mark was doing the right thing by helping the police to maintain law and order at a time when so-called left-wing loonies wanted anarchy.

The conversation returned to the subject of Frank and Ralph asked "What about Frank? How did that happen? Did you cross his palm with a motor? He was a guy with a pristine reputation until you got hold of him. I have seen him a couple of times during the strike and he's not the same. He's still a union official but that old sparkle has gone. Perhaps old age has crept up behind him, but I bet it's something to do with your bribe. Frank gave up on his principles and saved your guts in the process."

Mark's face hardened. He remained silent and, gulping down the remaining whiskey, rose from his chair to his full height, readjusted his belt as if he had put on a couple of extra pounds while drinking and announced: "Well, Ralph, what am I going to do with you? You are getting in the way. Perhaps I should not have said so much about my connections with the state. You know, they do pay well. Think of my second home at the seaside. Nice, isn't it?"

"Where's Sarah, by the way?" asked Ralph. "Your wife doesn't go out in an evening."

Mark: "She has tonight. The house is empty. Quite convenient, isn't it? No-one to eavesdrop, though you are never quite sure with the secret service. There could be a microphone under your chair."

Ralph became uneasy. He had not seen the dark side of Mark before. The darling of the left-wing activists walked over to a chest of drawers and slowly opened one. He gave Ralph a peculiar look, mocking him in his own inimitable mute fashion, and reached inside. To his horror Ralph realised that he was holding a revolver. Not an ordinary one at that. It looked like the one found at Jimmy's house then handed over to the police as evidence in the Bobby Lee case.

"What are you going to do with that gun?" he asked, trying to keep his nerve. "You do not intend to use that, do you? That's just being stupid – you have had too much to drink. Where did you get that? It's supposed to be in the possession of the police."

"I knew a cop at the police station. Handed it over for a few quid. No one noticed it had gone. Everyone thought the case would never be solved and that there would be no closure. After a few years the police forgot there was a gun involved in what was an old investigation."

Mark spun the chamber like a cowboy in a western film -the smooth, metallic clicking sound made Ralph feel anxious- and said: "No, this time you are okay. There's no ammunition or otherwise you would be a dead.

"I could have buried you in the bunker. That would have started another mysterious murder hunt. Your former boss is the only person who knows you are here, and it would not be difficult to knock him off – he's already half dead. It would become another mystery which would attract the attention of newspapers for years. Bobby Lee rides again, read all about it!

"Shooting you would be a suitable end for a deadbeat character. You do not realise, Ralph, that's my real opinion of you, do you? No ambition. No push. Always backing off from upsetting anyone in print. I am surprised Joan ever took you on.

"What would you think if I said I had given her one? What do you think about that? She said you were no good at that kind of thing."

He gazed at Ralph's downtrodden face, adding: "Do not worry, little boy, it never happened. I just wanted to get my pound of flesh since you have upset me tonight. Why do you want to destroy an old friend's career?"

"What about you, the great MP? You destroyed your career by selling your soul years ago. I have not sold mine – not yet."

"I had no choice when the government men came to see me. You have a choice with your soul. In the eyes of the law, I have not really done anything wrong, so why destroy my reputation? The establishment will look after its own and I'll get another job. Just a few old miners will refuse to speak to me. That's all."

Ralph could not take anymore. Mark's thoughts were becoming irrational and the quicker he got out before some rounds of ammunition were found the better.

"You know, Mark, I should not have listened to your father. He said that Jones that bleeding farmer was behind the black-market gang, and he was wrong. Mary Elliott told the truth – the villains were the Pinder family – and I did not believe her because I thought she was mad. It's a crazy world."

Ralph rose without saying goodnight and walked out of the room, leaving his former pal slumped in his chair. Mark, his mind befuddled by the alcohol and the verbal exchanges of the night, tried to grasp what would happen and thought in a hazy way there would be a banner headline, an excruciating story in the Advertiser and the disclosure of his resignation as MP in the subsequent edition.

Walking down the drive, Ralph had second thoughts about heading home and returned to the house, opening the front door without knocking and walking into the room where Mark had nodded off with a crooked smile.

Ignoring his woozily indisposed ex-pal, Ralph peered at the wall instead and announced: "I forgot to tell you. I got to know before leaving home. You are unaware of what's happened because the television has not been switched on tonight and you have not been answering phone calls. It looks like the strike is coming to an end."

Mark never heard him. He slumbered on, the crystal tumbler having slipped out of his right hand onto the thick carpet. The contents left behind a nasty stain like the comments that were exchanged that evening. He did not know what had happened in the coalfields until he came round with a king-size hangover in the morning.

A prickly atmosphere developed in the office over the next few days. Don was avoiding the golden boy who had mysteriously turned his back on the best story of the year. He was unable to understand why no copy was filed about Mark's shadowy world during the strike. Another great story had evaporated, and he was not speaking to his prodigy.

It was Ralph's yarn, through-and-through – it would not have materialised had it not been for his investigations - and Don, now part-time and with no authority, could no longer make sure it was printed. But the younger man's capitulation rankled with the old newshound. Not that he welched on Ralph to the Editor: "I am no grass," he told his mates.

Chapter 21

One afternoon Ralph's phone rang for the 20th time that day. At the end of the line was Joan. This time she was the controlling career woman rather than lover, and she was at her newspaper's London office. Like one of her crisp introductory sentences to a story, she came to the point straight away.

"Have you heard, Ralph?"

"What?" he replied bluntly.

She was the last person he wanted to talk to that morning. The mayor was being elusive about a scandal at his after-hours annual party at the town hall. A middle-aged council officer and his young secretary, inebriated by a bumper offering of free spirits in the mayor's comfy parlour, were caught making love in the dimly lit council chamber down the corridor. The news had leaked out.

"Mark has gone missing. It's a big story in London. He's not at home down here or at parliament. Our newspaper has been hunting him all over the place and Scotland Yard has issued an appeal for his whereabouts since his family are worried about his mental state."

Ralph: "Another escapologist. First Bobby Lee

now Mark. Both with connections to Two Trees. That house is jinxed. When are you going to vanish?"

"Be careful what you wish for," came the sharp reply.

"Let's get back to reality. Have you seen him? Have you quizzed him about those allegations that he's a union mole? It doesn't seem like it because I have not seen any follow-up stories in the left-wing newspapers. Sorry, the one left wing newspaper. Why didn't you press home the allegations against him? Has the Advertiser suddenly gone soft on its pals? Or has Don got something to do with it. I never trusted him deep down since he was too close to the community and there were too many of his pals destined not to be ruffled by bad publicity."

There were times when even her hard side softened; she did not wait for an answer as her boss was pushing her to embark on another assignment.

"I am going. Love you – we'll meet up soon, very soon, that's for certain," she told Ralph. "Soon, soon. I hope. I do miss you and we are still kindred spirits. Bye."

Ralph went to Mark's house. He was still on good terms with his wife and wanted to console her rather than dig for more information, for ferreting out personal details about people was becoming tiresome. The house looked abandoned, his wife having decamped to their daughter's home on the south coast to avoid the media circus, and he returned to the office.

Cars overloaded with national newspaper

reporters were now heading towards Yorkshire. One group was travelling north from London on the case of the runaway MP, which was seen as worthy material for elite journalists, and others from Manchester, where the northern editions of Fleet Street newspapers were printed, and where the reporters did not have the same pedigrees as their colleagues in the capital.

The foot-in-the-door lads from Lancashire, who were given the routine but tough job of finding the copulating civic couple, were told they had fled the town.

At the town hall the mayor was said to be hiding behind the settee in his parlour while a pack of ill-tempered reporters gathered at reception. All of them were muttering about the hellish conditions they had endured while driving over the foggy moors and several attired in sheepskin-coats were complaining about their feeble expenses. For the time being their minds were not on work.

That Friday was not a full working day for Ralph. He knew several of the national reporters wanted to pump him for information about the two scandals and at lunchtime he approached The Penny Farthing for a break.

Before entering he looked through a window and spotted a pair of hacks drinking wearily at the bar. One was London-based, a Cambridge graduate, and he looked out of his depth, Ralph later learning he did not even know Mark's wife had moved south. As Don had told him it was no good excelling at writing if you had no material on which to base a story.

To complicate matters for the outsiders, local party officials and councillors were abiding about the town's no-grassing culture – for the time being – and Ralph's local knowledge was much in demand by the so-called highfliers.

After switching to the down-market hostelry next door to avoid them, he had a couple of pints of lager on his own and thought about Mark, Joan and the good times. He was beginning to evolve into another Don: the past meant more than the contemporary news scene.

He was pleased that he had not pursued the MP over the allegations that he had been colluding with the establishment during the miners' strike, since punishing a friend was unforgivable, even though Mark had betrayed his family and the treasured union. Derek Lee, Bobby's son, had been right. He had walked away from the big scoop at the last minute.

As for Joan, he still pined and despite strenuous efforts to create new romances he had never topped that contradictory mix of contentment and exhilaration attained in their relationship during the early days at the newspaper. There was no one like her. He even missed, in a strange way, her explosive outbursts.

Three days later she phoned again and soon more revelations were fizzing around his mind. Mark had been tracked down to Australia where, having booked into a luxury hotel in Sydney, he went for a swim on a secluded beach and never returned.

"I am going to Australia to see what's happening," said Joan. "What do you think? I'm on top of the world again. It's a long way from writing the results of the egg and spoon race at a gala in Northfield. Do you recall how I rebelled and told Don he was an old fuddy-duddy for insisting the newspaper published such rubbish. Have you divorced him yet? See you, darling; I'll send a postcard from Australia. Lots of kisses.

"Oh, before I go. We are ahead of everyone else on this story but it's such a big one that we won't be able to keep it to ourselves and it will be all over the television screens tonight. Also, what's all this about the mayor and a scandal at the town hall? Who is he? It's not that blasted ex-miner from Broadway, is it? The one who told blue jokes in front of an audience including the Bishop of Wakefield.

Ralph smiled to himself. "No, it's not him. This one is left wing, teetotal and a puritan. Trust the treacherous side of life to push him into a situation like this, having to explain to the media why everyone got boozed up on the rates when all the staff had gone home. And then why two of the guests became intimate in the council chamber.

"I do not think he really wanted a party, not in his character, but it's a traditional part of town hall life and the other councillors wanted their ration of free booze.

"The amorous ructions could be heard two rooms away and a few of the boozy guests gathered around the entrance to the council chamber to listen to the noises coming from inside. It seems there were lots of gasps, grunts and giggles. Others stayed in the parlour pretending not to know what was happening. Not the mayor's fault of course but the public won't like it."

Her final words on the phone: "Bye. See you next time, darling. Get Don's desk ultra polished for my visit. It's still there, isn't it? Do not tell me that's gone as well. Everything is changing again."

Ralph laughed: "No, no it's there. Still in pristine condition for the benefit of lovers."

The story concerning Mark's vanishing act monopolised television and newspapers for weeks but, like Bobby Lee's disappearance, became stale news and the world moved on. The mayoral scandal was a one-day wonder that ruined two people's careers.

Joan returned from down under with little new information and went back to her desk in London, after which she chased dodgy rumours about dodgy celebrities, the new name of the game in the realms of newspapers. The work was boring and her mind drifted north.

Ralph answered the phone one evening while watching television in his new home, a terraced house near the Advertiser's offices. He had turned into a dowdy single man happy with his own company and a ballooning waistline

A woman's voice declared: "Chrysanthemums, incurved: 1, Jack Jones; 2, Margaret Thatcher; 3,

Adolf Hitler. Guess who?"

"No idea," he answered, smiling, and thinking of the old days when he typed out the results of the local flower show on his battered typewriter. Don insisted that every word and comma was correct or there were seismic explosions in the office. "How are you, Joan?"

Disillusioned with life in the metropolis, she was thinking of moving back to the wasteland, Northfield, and live with her one and only love, the dashing Ralph Baines, who had once been the Bain of her life. Both laughed.

"You are never out of my mind for long," she confided. "You return even at night while I'm sleeping. A comforting soul who enters my dreams and leaves me warm and safe."

"What's wrong, Joan? Fallen out of love with your profession? You were supposed to be pouring your energy into the job so you would become a distinguished international correspondent, whizzing from one continent to another in search of the big stories."

Joan: "Life is never what you expect, is it? Even Northfield looks like a shining beacon on the horizon these days, but I am convinced that within two weeks of being there I'd be screaming to get out and back to the bright lights. Even your marvellous company wouldn't lift my spirits. "

Ralph: "You have not found Mark, then?"

Joan: "No trace. The sharks must have got him. There was a former Prime Minister of Australia who did the same thing. Went for a swim and did not come back. I met one of his friends while I was over there investigating Mark's disappearance. The man is convinced the Prime Minister was picked up by a submarine and whisked to China following accusations he was spying for them. He's sure the politician is alive. A case of deep denial on the friend's part, I am afraid."

Ralph: "Similar to Mark's case except that our man was spying for the British government during the strike and not for the Chinese or Russians. Don has a theory though - he believes Mark is living under an assumed name in Darwin."

Joan: "Is that old goat still alive? How does a daft man like him know? Haven't you two got divorced yet?"

Ralph quipped: "Just a legal separation", adding: "He's retired full time, but I go to see him and his wife at home. Their Glenys makes beautiful French toast. Slices of thick white bread soaked in Yorkshire Pudding batter and fried in hot fat. Golden slices of hot bread; it's paradise on a budget. Don brews his own bitter and that's good as well. We have some delicious suppers in winter.

"I think Don is quite serious about the Darwin connection. He says a branch of the Pinder family settled in Darwin at the end of the second world war and came over for a holiday in this country during the 1950s. The newspaper did a big story about it. Local man makes good in Australia and all that and lots of quotes were printed relating to the old days in

Northfield before the family emigrated.

"Don said Mark, then a young man, was impressed by what they all said about life over there and wanted to emigrate. He got a passport and there was an offer of a job. However, he married, had kids and a life in politics beckoned in Northfield. Don wrote the stories, so he knows all about the visit by the Aussie branch of the Pinders."

Joan: "What does Don know about anything? Never had any time for him. He ought to be burning in hell at the crematorium."

Ralph defended his friend by saying he had been his mentor, a fine teacher who got him off the hook in his early days when he had dropped a clanger by upsetting a local worthy. A few words from Don to the angry man and the contentious issue disappeared. He never heard another word of complaint.

"Not sure how he did it, but he did. In many ways he kept the newspaper from falling apart in the old days. Solid as rock."

Joan: "That's you as well. I always said you were like a rock. You never wavered. A wonderful characteristic. Not like poor old me, too capricious for that kind of thing. I change my mind every day. I have a rotten temper as well. Sometimes I wonder why you bother with me."

One evening life became complicated again. At home he was thinking of Joan, her erratic ways and his loneliness when there was a knock on the front door. He looked at his watch, realised it was late and decided to give the visitor a rollicking, especially if it was someone wanting an item of low-grade news in the newspaper. Having to live in the town where you worked as a reporter had its disadvantages.

On opening the door, he was surprised to find Betty, whom he had not seen for months. She was fresh faced, had lost a little weight and her expensive clothes suggested a new boyfriend. In the living room she demanded a divorce so she could remarry.

"I do not want any fuss or tantrums," she added, breathing deeply to strengthen her resolve and suppress tears, for there was a residue of emotion retained for her husband. "I just want to get married. Do you understand?"

Her fingers moved perpetually, first clenching a tissue on her lap and then releasing it, and her head was bowed in despair. He felt sorry but there was no chance of a reconciliation.

"I'll do whatever you ask," he replied, calmly. He had never loved her, having sleepwalked into the marriage, believing that he could not leave it too late, or people would start questioning his sexuality. It had not been a bad married life but lacked excitement and passion, two components of a modern relationship which Joan had amply supplied. There was no going back.

Betty said her boyfriend, Dave, was a good man who would add stability to her life, unlike Ralph whom she now realised was a waste of time and whose daft job had turned him into an irredeemable rogue.

"In the old days I told my friends I wanted my

children to grow up to be like you, Ralph. Good and thoughtful, a gentleman, but you turned out to be a lecherous sod and I hope you rot in hell. You need passion like some people need drugs; I need a stability and a family life."

At that juncture she rose, threw the damp and crumpled tissue into his face and stormed out of the house, slamming the front door. Ralph winced, hoping the old walls and ceiling would withstand the violent vibration and thankful he was stonily immune to her emotional storm. He could thank Joan and her chaotic love life for his thick hide.

Three days later Joan phoned again and put forward a proposition. Her bank balance was ballooning like his waistline and her stalker, the tax man, was hovering near the front door and she wanted to spend money. That included taking Ralph on all-expenses long break to Australia, visiting the cities and tourist sites.

"I want a holiday of a lifetime, "she announced, gleefully. "Oh dear, that's the kind of old-fashioned phrase Don used in his stories. In his day Palma was a holiday of a lifetime. In our case, the holiday will live-up to the hackneyed phrase; in fact, it will be mind- blowing. We'll get to know each other again before it's too late. I want a holiday to escape from London. Who said if you are tired of London, you are tired of life? Go on tell me, you are good at that kind of thing."

"Dr Samuel Johnson, "he replied pretentiously, as if appearing on University Challenge, and added:

"This fancy holiday down under? It has got nothing to do with the disappearance of Mark, has it?"

"We are going to Alice Springs not Darwin and it's nothing to do with him. I have had a belly full of Mr Pinder, MP. Also, I would not spend a penny on a tip from that old fool, Don. At least you'll get away from him for a while. Fancy that, divorce at last. It's quite simple on my part - I am tired of London, and we are going. Just kick over the traces for once, Ralph."

His reply: "What do you mean 'going' ..is it booked?"

"Yes."

"Well, that's it then. I'll pack my bags and tell Don. He will be pleased. Perhaps not. Perhaps peeved. I do not think he has ever stepped out of this country. Their holidays were always spent in Bournemouth."

Part three
Chapter 22
The year, 1986

They were on the BA flight to Sydney when Ralph, breaking the tedium, spoke about the mysterious disappearance of a couple of prominent politicians over the years. One of them faked his own death and was tracked down to Australia, where he was living under a false identity with his secretary. Ralph thought Mark could well have done the same. After all, he was a strong swimmer, and no-one saw him go under in the sea.

Joan, whose mind was deep in a newspaper, glanced momentarily at the countless faces in the rows of seats and wondered how many were also on a holiday of a lifetime, recalling Don's antiquated term, and then focused on Ralph, hoping he would shut up so she could continue reading.

He was by nature a reticent man but since boarding the plane at Heathrow Airport in London he had been talking about a plethora of stories and experiences that were interesting at first. The persistent mental pummelling, however, made her tetchy and she wondered what had overcome him.

His escape from Northfield had turned him into a compulsive talker.

"Do you recall, Joan, an MP called John Stonehouse who was a former member of the Labour cabinet?"

"I remember him, but I am not strong on details on the grounds I did not cover the story," she replied half-heartedly, knowing he would produce a library of facts that would scramble her brain and take her mind off the impending excitement of Australia.

Ignoring her inattention, he continued with the monologue, revealing that Stonehouse, who had financial difficulties, went for a swim on a beach in Miami, America, in 1974. Leaving behind a pile of clothes on a beach, it was presumed he had drowned. Newspapers even printed his obituary in good faith.

The runaway MP and his secretary were later traced to Australia, where the police at first thought he was another fugitive from justice, Lord Lucan, who had disappeared a fortnight earlier. The politician was convicted of fraud and sentenced to seven years in prison.

"The other was the man you have mentioned before, Harold Holt, a Prime Minister in Australia in the 1960s," Ralph continued." He went swimming in rough seas at Portsea, Victoria, and was never seen again. He was on holiday with no bodyguard. Amazing, really.

"He probably drowned as he was not in the best of health and his doctor a few days earlier had told him not to overexert himself while swimming. No body was found. As you have said, there have been a lot of conspiracy theories including one that he had been a spy for the Chinese government and that he had been taken away in a submarine."

On terminating his monologue, he said: "Wouldn't it be lovely if Mark was still alive, living in obscurity and then we found him. The look on his chubby face. It would be a pure delight and a sight to behold, worth the 12,000-mile journey. Then there would be the pleasure of seeing him banged up in prison.

"Do you realise that a scoop like that would make you a household name? People would be talking about the intrepid woman reporter who ensnared the runaway politician for decades. Remember, Joan, fame is your spur. Howard Spring and all that.

"Who was Howard Spring?"

Ralph muttered through his teeth that he was a novelist who wrote a bestselling novel, Fame is the Spur, about an idealist MP who became a Prime Minister and was subsequently corrupted by power and money.

"Where were you educated?" he asked, giving her a counterfeit black look. "It can't have been a finishing school. More like a council primary."

She retorted: "Listen to the kettle telling the frying pan it's black. I know, I know. Cliché, cliché. Get lost, darling - that's another cliché."

Pausing for breath, he motored on with his obsessive stories. A woman sitting nearby, readjusting her reading spectacles at the end of her nose, turned, and glanced at Joan in sympathy, believing she was handling her companion's verbal attrition so well.

"I think Mark was a good swimmer at school and won a few medals and silver shields in competitions, so it's unlikely he drowned. I went through all the old files at the newspaper and there was quite a lot of material about his swimming prowess."

She looked upwards in despair: "We are going on a holiday, remember? I am not going looking for him; he's probably been devoured by sharks and is now an intrinsic ingredient in a fish soup served in a Chinese restaurant in Sydney. I just hope his bony bits don't get caught in a customer's teeth. That's all. Just because Don has mentioned Darwin, you have become fixated on his theory. Your boss can't be right. Or does he possess a crystal ball?"

On becoming petulant, he replied: "Do not underestimate Don. I remember in the 1960s when he was the only person in the office who thought there was a connection between Two Trees and the disappearance of Bobby Lee. Everyone had a good laugh behind his back. Afterwards everything fell into place and Don concluded he could see into the future. He was joking of course but you never know with him. He's not what you think he is. Never has been.

"I recall in the early years when there was an accident at a pit and two men were killed. The national newspaper reporters headed straight to our office for information. The National Coal Board's press officers were holding back the names and addresses for some reason and the big-wig newsmen were impatient.

"The reporters were complaining like mad. Don told them we were having trouble getting the information as well. He never trusted press officers because he believed they were employed to withhold information and tell lies if necessary. He knew the pit manager's secretary, phoned her, got the names and addresses and sent the lot by phone to the Manchester offices.

"When the high-class reporters phoned their bosses with the news that they were still waiting for the names, they were rudely told that they were useless and that a good operator from Northfield had done the work more efficiently. Don earned a few bob that day and the secretary received a bottle of wine in appreciation."

"So sorry," Joan replied, without any emotion but continued reading while giving him an unsubtle warning: "We are not going after red herrings in Darwin, not likely. No ferreting in bars looking for a sad VIP from Northfield. There's no time for wild goose chases."

Ralph laughed: "You have spent too much on the tabloids, Joan. Red herrings? Wild goose chase? What would your tutors near the Swiss lakes say? More cliches, dear. Don would not like it either."

Joan: "There you go again. That name. Don this, Don that. You remember the egg and spoon race results many years' ago? 1,2,3?"

"How can I forget them?" he replied, as though recalling romantic sunsets but inside he was laughing.

Joan: "If I hear that name again on this holiday, it will be a case of 1,2,3, and you'll be thrown off this plane at 30,000 feet or whatever. No parachute and no Don to soften your crash landing. From now on I'm going to call him Donald. It fits. As in Donald Duck. Please, please, Ralph, get some sleep."

He was not giving up – not yet at least.

"How do you know about Donald Duck cartoons? Girls who attend finishing school don't watch that stuff."

She almost exploded in frustration: "If you really want to know, my mother and I slipped out of the house in an evening to watch them at the cinema in Northfield. Are you satisfied?"

Declining to reply, he motored on: "You have heard of Hanging Rock, haven't you?"

"What? What is it? Tell me and shut up. You are wearing out my nerves. "

Disregarding her hectoring and, having enjoyed winding her up while she was immersed in a newspaper, he went on: "Can you recall the Australian film, 'Picnic at Hanging Rock? A group of schoolgirls went for a picnic on a summer's day in 1900 and disappeared. It was supposed to have been based on a true story, but people are not sure. A great film, made in 1979 and ahead of its time. You see people are always vanishing in Australia."

"Really? Joan replied, sadly.

"Then there is Victor," he said, relishing her sombre look.

"Victor, Victor who?" she asked loudly, her eyes widening, and two rows of mean narrow eyes focused on them, willing the couple to shut up.

"Victor Grayson, an MP in Colne Valley in my neck of the woods. He disappeared in 1920. In London, however, not in Australia. No trace. Special Branch thought he was a spy for the Russians or the IRA. More resourceful than our Mark who spied for our government. How can you spy for your own government in your own country?"

"Go to sleep."

The plane was heading into the night and the lights in the cabin dimmed to signify people were to remain quiet save for the occasional whisper. Ralph relented and his comments dried up.

"Whoopee," a chorus of nearby passengers retorted loudly, welcoming the sudden halt to the monotonous dialogue. Other dozing passengers were less polite.

The much-anticipated wondrous holiday was not evolving as planned and the newspaper slipped from her hands onto the floor, and she gazed around the anonymous faces in the subdued lighting in the plane in a dreamy attempt to switch off from him.

Hurry on Sydney, the heat, Bondi Beach and roof top garden bars, she concluded. How could she decouple him from his preoccupation with the mysterious disappearances of once vaunted people? Why couldn't he embrace the exhilaration of a holiday? A free one at that.

Chapter 23

Two days later in Sydney the roaring surf, the sea food on platters and crisp wine from the Blue Mountains performed their magic. Yet another Ralph emerged from his chrysalis, and she marvelled at his gusto as he absorbed the night life in a non-stop frenzy of fun. Twenty years of suppressing excitement in the interests of decorum in the office had built up pressure inside him and the dam wall gave way as he tasted freedom.

In comparison Joan, once the darling of the clubs in London, appeared to be a maiden aunt.

The former loner who spent evenings watching television and drinking with his equally dowdy mates at The Butchers was now a cool character, each evening wearing a smart lightweight suit, well cut by his bespoke tailor back in Northfield.

He ditched the suit and his sunny charm in the day and a newly acquired wardrobe of brightly coloured beachwear and loud t-shirts turned him into a caricature of a rowdy Australian. He soon realised most of the residents were not like that at all but did not change his new persona which he enjoyed.

She could not restrain him and feared he had

gone too far in the opposite direction, having turned into a human tornado who swept through night clubs with impunity.

"You have finally thrown off your Northfield shackles," she told him, not convinced she liked the new man.

A quick tour of the opera house in Sydney was followed by a visit to the Blue Mountains, where the remarkable blue haze lingering over the valleys was memorable and the local wine even more memorable. More than anything else they enjoyed meeting Australians – most of whom, thankfully, were not boorish and more interesting than the lads back home.

Having met in a bar a jolly man who had worked as a reporter on Australian evening newspapers, then sheared sheep on one of the vast ranches in the Northern Territory, Ralph concluded that adventure had been sadly lacking in his life.

After a couple of whirlwind weeks they were off to Adelaide, with Ralph beginning to wonder where all the money was coming from, but they ploughed on, and Joan never mentioned the budget which appeared to be inexhaustible. In Adelaide they proposed to spend a few days hoovering up the sights before boarding a train to the ultimate destination, Alice Springs.

He never mentioned anyone back home and became absorbed in landscapes, cityscapes and the characters they met on the way.

At the same time their relationship began to evolve into something new, displaying a deep sense of belonging to each other that had not always been prevalent in the past.

One evening she became romantic over several glasses of white wine: "You still have not said it. The one thing that would make me a complete woman."

"What's that?" he asked, apparently nonplussed.

"You know what I mean. You are playing games. Don't you remember those simple words: 'I love you.'

He refused to join in: "Why do I have to keep saying it? I told you how I felt years ago. Before you gave me the big heave and ran away. That's enough for me. In some ways I am continuing to suffer the fallout from that break-up; you'll have to wait. Next month perhaps."

She was crestfallen and changed the subject.

Within a month his fast living calmed down and she began to recognise the old Ralph again; it seemed fitting that his garish beachwear and the light-weight suit were packed away in readiness for the long journey home.

He asked one day why she had selected Alice Springs.

"It was Darwin or Alice Springs," she replied, on arrival at Alice. "I've been to the tourist areas and southern cities before and wanted to try to find the last vestiges of a frontier town in the Northern Territory and have a look at ancient Aboriginal culture. Not quite what I expected but it's different."

After breakfast at the hotel restaurant on the second day, and on returning to the bedroom, a letter was pushed under the door.

"What is it?" she asked.

He looked puzzled: "It is a hand-written note. I do not understand it. It has been pushed under the door by staff. The message says, 'Catch Me If You Can?" Very strange. I wonder whether it has been pushed under the wrong door. Oh dear, the post mark is Darwin.

"There are also two air tickets and the destination, surprise, surprise, is Darwin. On top of that the writer has mentioned a good hotel there. Very nice of them."

Joan: "I do not understand. What a peculiar message. Free tickets? What's all that about? Oh, well let's get going and have a walk down the street. See what's happening in a town called Alice."

He paused, deeply troubled. "It's about Mark. I just know. Gut instinct. I had forgotten about his grandfather's little introductory cards in the 1920s."

"Don't bring him up," she replied angrily. "You are trying to divert attention from the holiday. How can it be him? He's almost certainly dead. You haven't been in touch with Donald, have you? Donald Duck. It seems like one of his mad theories."

The letter's mysterious message analysed by agile minds that belied the age of the two journalists. Finally Joan, reluctantly turning her back on the holiday, said she had enough money to extend the visit to try to find out what was happening. The 800-mile flight to Darwin took two hours and halfway the consensus was they were probably chasing shadows with the detour bound to end in failure.

"Oh drat," she announced on landing. "I am having second thoughts about this expedition. We can't be on the right track, can we? Pure folly on our part. Look at what I have missed- never got round to seeing the site of the first Telegraph Office in Alice. It marks the site of the first European settlement in the area. Really wanted to see that. Never mind. "

He looked puzzled: "The Telegraph Office? What are you talking about? Small fry, isn't it? It's not The Eiffel Tower, is it? Not in the same tourist league. Are you serious?"

She smiled. Her eyes telegraphed the message that he was slow on the uptake sometimes and for once she was the joker.

"Within a couple of hours, I'll know whether there is a scent of a story here. If that's the case it will be all systems go. Otherwise, we'll go home. Simple as that."

She added: "What I do not understand is why Mark walked into the sea. He was following the same scenario as John Stonehouse. People were bound to be suspicious."

Ralph: "I think that's why he did it. People would not believe he would do something so daft and follow Stonehouse's route of escape. So, they believed he drowned. The main thing is that no-one has found a body. Not even a fastidious scoffer at a classy fish restaurant in Sydney."

In Darwin nothing happened out of the ordinary for two days as they waited for contact with the letter-writer. For a while the city seemed to be the most unexciting spot in the world. However, while walking out of the hotel on the third day, a middle-aged woman strode out in front of them, having emerged from a coffee bar next door. She wore a white t-shirt, matching shorts and a wide brim hat and continued to press ahead, striding out with all the poise of a model on the catwalk. So self-assured.

"Who is it?" asked Joan, having realised he was taking more than a casual interest in the woman. "Too old for you, Ralph. You do not fancy her, do you?

Again, he paused and gestured to his girlfriend to halt. She said: "What's wrong? You do fancy her. I pay for the holiday, and you set your sights on someone else. When will I learn?"

"I know her," came the reply. "I can't believe what's happening. Where's Mark?

"Who is it?"

"Mark's former friend, Janet. I think she wants us to follow her. She must have been sitting next to the window in the coffee shop, spotted us approaching and deliberately walked out to catch our attention."

They continued to pursue her, looking for accomplices but there weren't any.

"This heat is getting me down," moaned Joan, and his reply turned her face sullen: "Well you wanted to come. Just follow her and shut up."

For the next five minutes all three remained quiet as they strolled towards a multi storey car park where the woman halted and turned to face them: "Hello,

Ralph, how are you getting on? Nice to see you again. Fancy hunting us down after all this time."

He did not reply, wondering what to say next in this extraordinary situation. Joan was the first to break the silence: "Where's Mark? How did you know we were in Australia?"

Pointing to the multi storey, she said her car was parked on the third floor and everything would be explained at home. The bungalow was a situated a few miles beyond the city boundary and the journey would not take more than half an hour, she said.

Reluctantly the couple, who were supposed to be enjoying themselves, climbed into the Volvo estate and sped off through the city streets and beyond onto the highway in the direction of the Kakadu National Park. Joan smiled weakly and squeezed his hand on the back seat, not out of affection but because she needed his support, that rock-like strength that had never wavered in a crisis.

Janet never said a word, nor did she turn her head as she negotiated the traffic beyond the city's suburbs, the vehicle finally arriving at a modern bungalow that did not seem to be particularly imposing. Instead, it was the shady and tiered garden full of bright colours and the endless bush beyond that captured their attention.

"Won't you have a cup of coffee or tea or a glass of wine," Janet asked her guests as they sat in the living room, taking in the high-quality furniture, the highly polished grand piano in a recess and a series of old prints on the wall that looked valuable. A framed photograph of Mark lorded over the mantelpiece.

"Well, Ralph, haven't you anything to say for yourself?" said Janet, smiling. "I have never seen you tongue tied before

As usual Joan was first to talk: "I'll ask again. Where is Mark?"

"I am afraid Mark died a couple of months ago. He had a heart attack in the kitchen and died later in hospital."

Removing a photograph from her handbag, she handed it to Ralph, pointing out that that was his grave in the local cemetery.

"Trust Mark to die twice," said Ralph, forcing a grin. "He always had to be different."

The couple were sitting on a settee. Leaning over and placing her hand on his shoulder, Joan took a good look at the photograph. It showed a standard white gravestone with a sentimental inscription and the words: "Graham Docherty, January 25, 1930, to February 13, 1986" in distinctive black letters. Joan began to assemble questions.

Janet's face, which appeared to be devoid of emotion, led him to believe she did not seem to be a typical grieving partner. On cue her eyes watered. Glancing away from the couple, she said the past few months had been devastating and the fact there was no close family to offer support made the heavy burden more excruciating.

After extending his condolences, he paid tribute to his friend, but all the time thought they were all actors in a film drama rather than in real life. It was all so surreal. What was it all about? Joan, having corralled enough initiative to force a breakthrough, asked how their host had tracked them down.

Peering at Ralph as if he ought to know, Janet said it was down to the column that he wrote for the Advertiser every week.

"The Onlooker column?" he asked bewildered. "Are you joking? Come on? No, that can't be true. How ridiculous."

"Not Don's masterpiece of meaningless gung, is it?" interceded Joan, smiling to herself over the fact that he had taken over the infamous column, the office hoot.

He was not backing off a quarrel, his pride having been bruised: "Watch your English, young lady. Meaningless gung? Does that mean you can have meaningful gung? All gung is gung and meaningless."

Janet punctured the growing row between them by continuing: "More than a month ago you couldn't resist telling your hallowed readers that you were having the holiday of a lifetime. You went into detail, mentioning destinations and dates. You were showing off and explaining why your name would not appear at the bottom of the column for a long time.

"Later a stranger, a local man in a pub, asked questions about the holiday, having read your piece in the Advertiser, and you gave him everything he wanted to know. You did not realise what you were doing. Mark has close friends in Northfield. The information was sent to me after his death along with the newspaper cutting. That's it. It's that simple.

"I checked you out on arrival at the airport and tracked you both down in Alice by phoning hotels and asking for Mr and Mrs Baines, after which I posted the letter. It was easy, really. It could have been complicated had I been searching for the apocryphal Mr and Mrs Smith. I suppose those days have gone when single couples assumed counterfeit marital status to try to maintain an element of respectability. When are you going to get married? It's been going on for years. People are beginning to think there is something wrong with you both."

Joan could not resist ribbing him again about the column: "Well, well. You are just like Don. Donald Duck. 'Holiday of a lifetime'. Same cliché column, same kind of material. The column that time forgot. He glorified the parish pump standard of news and ignored the meaningful issues elsewhere in the locality. When taking over the column, I thought you would have injected style into what should be the showpiece feature of the newspaper. Ralph, you are a dead loss."

Janet rescued him from his red-faced predicament by saying she had something uncomfortable to reveal, a decision she had not taken half-heartedly, and which had caused sleepless nights.

"I want to reveal the full story. Go public. Our escape from the UK, the fake death on the beach near

Sydney and our hideaway in Darwin under false names. Everything that happened in our topsy-turvy world, carbuncles and all, and I would like to be paid handsomely for the disclosures. Very handsomely. Or there is no deal. I'll go elsewhere to the highest bidder."

She hesitated and looked apologetically at Ralph. She realised his newspaper was financially incapable of meeting the bill, but Joan was a different proposition since her proprietors boasted a big cheque book, which could make life bearable for her over a few years.

"Mark and I were struggling towards the end of his life. Getting out of the UK with the help of his shadowy friends in the government was expensive and we were living on handouts from the branch of his family who settled in Darwin. They never seemed to mind that he was a man on the run; I think they enjoyed the notoriety and never said a word to anyone else.

"We were in a wonderful country, full of sunshine and adventure, and we were recluses, too frightened to venture out of doors and having to rely on family."

Back at the hotel the couple indulged in a brainstorming session and the rest of the holiday was emphatically forgotten. So were the defects inherent in the poor old Onlooker column, now a forbidden topic. They were back at work, absorbed in each other's company as in the dreary little office back home, and there was no time for regrets.

"I'm going back to see her," she insisted. "I'll get her signed-up. My newspaper will send the cash so I can hang on here while I do the interviews and the writing. If her story is true, this will be a cracker, make a name for myself."

"Where do I fit in?" he asked, suspiciously. Hostility appeared in her eyes. It was triggered by her inveterate desire for finding a story and that addiction to the stimulus that came with brash headlines. He had seen that look many times in journalists working for national newspapers and never liked it.

"Oh, er, you'll have to return on the booked flight," she added. "You can't escape that. The newspaper wants you back, you've been away far too long. I'll stay here and we'll meet up later, perhaps in Northfield. I'll keep in touch on the phone. Is that all right with you, darling?

He replied: "I do not like what you are doing as you seem to be squeezing me out. You would not have ensnared this story without my assistance. Or Don's for that matter. We were the ones who kept on saying Mark had faked his death. You poo-pooed the lot. You wanted to study the Aboriginal culture and soak up the sun and the night life. Not that I haven't enjoyed myself at your expense. But now another side of your character has taken over.

"You have forgotten one thing, Joan."

"What's that?" she replied. He realised that he had lost her once again as she was heading off into that other land in her mind. The sensational story would occupy all her energy and time until the assignment was finished.

"The only way you can prove Mark is dead is by exhuming the body. There could be someone else in that coffin. Have you thought about that?"

"Yes, I have. We'll go ahead with the existing story, print the merry widow's version of events and see what happens. If they find the body of a tramp six feet under, all the better because it will be an even greater story. We'll hunt down Mark wherever he is."

He spent a minute staring at her while her back was turned. She was packing a suitcase.

"I think I have something to say," he said, quietly and apologetically. "Something special. Close to your heart. Three words. Magical words?"

"Oh, no," she replied, her heart hardening. "You are not getting round me that way. Times have changed. This is an inappropriate time for that kind of thing. Another place, another time. I can wait for 'I love you'. I have been patient and time is not a problem except when it comes to deadlines. You know how important they are to newspaper people. Shame on you."

He changed the topic: "I think you are like Runaround Sue."

Startled, she stopped packing: "Not another one. First Victor, the runaway MP, now Runaround Sue. Who is Runaround Sue? Tell me and then shut up."

"You would not know about her during your cloistered life in The Alps. It was the title of a hit record by Dion in 1961. Runaround Sue tied up lads in emotional chaos then ran off to find a new victim.

I think they call that kind of girl a…"

She hurled the suitcase onto the floor.

"Do not dare say that term in my presence! Two can play at that game. Viva Las Vegas, so there. Elvis Presley, 1967."

"What's so special about that?"

"Nothing at all. But that's where I am going after receiving my bonus for this exclusive. So there. This time without a scrounger exploiting my goodwill – you would spend all the money on one-armed bandits. Instead you'll have to make do with the slot machines at Cleethorpes while I am living it up."

"Well," he replied, forcing a smile. "This is a typical episode in the lives of Ralph and Joan incorporated. One minute we are in paradise, the next thrashing each other. Better get moving, catch the plane and head back to the sleepy old Advertiser. Stabbed in the back again."

"Cliché!" she snorted. "Stabbed in the back, indeed."

Chapter 24

On returning to Northfield he discovered the aftermath of a bout of backstabbing in the office. The Editor, made redundant at the grand old age of 59, had been replaced by a dapper whizzkid, a relative newcomer to the town. His aim was to revamp what the owners thought was a Victorian attitude towards news and guide the newspaper towards the twenty first century. Local news for local people was on its way out.

The incoming boss was bulky with a crop of black curls and large angry eyes that bored through you like a laser. He had worked for a few months on a national newspaper at its Manchester offices, a job that impressed the Advertiser's gullible proprietors who thought they had a Pulitzer Prize writer on their hands.

"What do you do?" he asked at their first meeting, and that was followed by a sly glance implying Ralph was masquerading as a reporter. He was not pleased that a member of staff had taken what appeared to be an endless holiday on the other side of the world.

Ralph, realising that he may well have been

placed on the danger list as far as the job was concerned, said this-and-that, pointing out he enjoyed sniffing around the streets and pubs – often in his own time – searching for off-beat stories. He thought the readers had survived for too long on a stodgy diet of council stories and word-for-word reports at the magistrates' court.

"If you want good stories you must talk to people at venues where they meet in numbers. The pub is a perfect place. That's where the real stuff is. You must break away from solicitors, councillors and community leaders who live in a bubble that's beyond the real lives of ordinary people.

"Our readers like stories about babies, animals and people who make them laugh. Give them that nutritious diet every week and the circulation will bloom. Otherwise, it's the gallows for the Advertiser – it will go out of business in 20 years."

"Very interesting," the newcomer declared, already weary at the presence of someone who could become an undesirable influence in his new look office. "But I am not convinced. You need an office diary and loads of assignments to keep everyone busy and then you select the best stories that are produced by the reporters. We do not have the time to look for your version of news. Modern weekly newspapers have deadlines to meet and a conveyor belt approach is required to keep everyone busy. Busy, busy, that's what I like. Nose to the grindstone."

His adversary peered at the ceiling, muttering to himself that the clichés that had haunted the lives of

Don and Joan's lecturers in Switzerland were once again running rampant. Poor old Don had wasted 30 years trying to eradicate the little blighters, only for them to reappear like mice when no-one was looking.

Dick, the new boss, blatantly lacked imagination. He continued: "From now, Ralph, you'll cover the town hall and keep an eye on what the police and fire brigade are up to. Splendid. Suuuu-per."

Ralph had one consolation. Dick's Christian name soon earned a sobriquet that was not to be mentioned to his face. Without any effort on his part, Dick had taken over Don's role as the office joke but without his predecessor's hidden talents including forecasting the future with uncanny accuracy.

Gazing upwards again, having realised the new man was another plastic nondescript, Ralph continued sarcastically: "You like the content that my pals in the tap room will find a riveting read. Such as Councillor Rhubarb's exhilarating rhetoric on the tribulations of beautifying civic parks. How to bore our readership in 40 pages of solid and putrefying type. Broadsheet pages not tabloid of course.

Ralph ended the conversation by mocking the new tyrant's favourite words: "Splendid. Suuuu-per."

With the phone ringing, Ralph picked up the receiver without realising what he had done, and that made him wince since it was apparent that repetitive unthinking tasks and over identification with the job were turning him into a zombie.

"Hello, darling," drooled the voice at the end of

the line in Australia. Joan was on form, exuberantly so, for she could not wait to tell him about her interviews down under. Her newspaper was poised to send the exclusive yarn around the world. In minute detail, she went through what she had been told and thought Mark's partner was basically a trustworthy person who had no axe to grind and who just wanted money. She was already haggling for a down payment, an advance, Joan said.

At the end of her monologue he waited for his moment of opportunity, a move that would wipe the sneer off Dick's face on the grounds he would announce to the office the biggest story since the disappearance of dear old Bobby Lee. It would fill that week's front page.

Ralph asked her: "When do we get our chance at this story? You are not going to keep it all to yourself, are you? Can we be first? A splash lead on our front page at the Advertiser would not make any difference to a global enterprise like your outfit. An executive in London or New York is not bothered about what happens on a newspaper in Northfield."

There was a long pause at the other end of the line, and he changed course: now he knew what was coming: a bucket full of excuses which meant he was on his own.

"We do sell 35,000 copies on a good day in Northfield," she replied, trying to wriggle out of any dubious commitments made in the past. "That's a lot, nearly as many as your bellyache of a newspaper in a week. My boss wants this story exclusive, with no exemptions even for the Advertiser."

Ralph: "That's not fair. You would not have got the story without me. Even Don played his part. He had a gut instinct Mark and his lady were heading to Darwin."

Then he switched topics.

"Oh, you do not know, do you? I have sad news. I am sorry to say Don died while we were on holiday. I tried to contact him by phone on arriving home and his wife told me. Really bad news: I had worked with him for years; a great man and you could not buy his experience.

"The poor man was buried alive at the newspaper aged 18. Metaphorically speaking of course. Just went to work, then home, sometimes via the pub. He lived in a bubble for decades. Spent years looking forward to retirement and on walking down Church Street for the final time discovered he could not live without the office. Went to pieces and his health deteriorated. Who wants to end like that?

"Anyway, what would he think about his best journalist double crossing his newspaper?"

Quick to retaliate and unaffected by the sad news, she said: "Don never gave me a second thought. All he thought about was you and his pals who had status in the community."

"That's not fair," he retorted, defending himself and his old boss once again. "Mark's girlfriend would not have recognised you coming out of the hotel in Darwin. She's never seen you before. I met her on numerous occasions. Mind you, I never realised there was something between them - he always seemed so faithful to his wife. Silly me. I was too close to see the truth."

He was about to launch into another diatribe when the line went dead, and he put down the receiver slowly: his mind had switched off from life for a few moments.

"It's time you went to the town hall – there's a meeting of the general purposes committee at 4pm," an irritated, gruff voice announced from the same desk where Don had spent too many years worrying about deadlines. Within a few seconds Ralph, compliant for a change, was on his way to listen to an afternoon of municipal drivel.

Another of Ralph's tasks in the new all dancing, all singing regime in the office was to open the mail, which in former years had been the responsibility of the Editor's secretary or the youngest reporter on the payroll.

"This is all gunge," he muttered to Richard, the new young reporter who was already beginning to think that Ralph was a phantom from the past, someone to avoid since he had no idea about modern journalism or what made a good story. How wrong he was.

"Ninety per cent of the letters are from public relation firms wanting a free plug in the local newspaper," said Ralph. "This one is even worse. It's from the local nutter. Look at the spidery writing. Dear oh dear he's predicting an earthquake in Northfield at midnight tonight. Makes a change from the volcano that was going to erupt in Locke Park last year."

The next envelope lifted him from his gloom and on recognising the handwriting glanced around to make sure Richard was not watching. To his relief the new junior was engrossed in rewriting a press release from the council.

After opening the envelope, he found a card similar in size to the type handed out to contacts by businessmen. Richard glanced at it but did not take any more notice and continued typing. Ralph, however, realised what was happening – it was identical to the one delivered to him in Australia.

'Catch Me If You Can' it announced in small italics. Its significance was anything but small and the card was placed into his wallet. It had a local postmark.

So, he's alive, is he? Ralph smiled, thankful in a strange way that the fugitive had evaded his pursuers once again and that Joan was about to publish a story that could be out-of-date within hours. 'Catch Me If You Can', what's he up to?

One thing was for certain: he wasn't going to tell Dick about this new mystery and walked out of the office determined not to carry out his assignment that day – covering meetings at the dreaded town hall. The municipal cretins were out-of-bounds for him that day.

"Where are you going?" demanded the voice that seemed to be impregnated with gravel and vindictiveness. "Aren't you supposed to be covering…"

Disregarding the odious windbag, he continued out of the building and went down the street, having decided to try to meet the absentee MP. Where was he?

There was one possible solution. In his early political career Mark always had a pint of beer with him on a Friday evening in Florrie's bar at the Queens where they talked politics. Both felt at ease there, unencumbered by the presence of bosses and men in suits. Later the politician's high-flying friends said the low life bar was not good for his image and the meetings were terminated.

"Also get rid of your dead-beat reporter pal from the local rag – there are more important scribes in London," he was told, but Mark ignored that bit of advice.

Ralph proposed to stay in the renamed Penny Farthing for a few hours every evening until the politician walked in. Until then, he had a problem with his new boss who was demanding to know why he had left the office in a paddy and why he had not covered the job that had been assigned to him on the sacrosanct office diary.

"I couldn't be bothered," he told Dick, bluntly, and the other reporters in the office turned in disbelief. The typewriters stopped churning out copy for a few seconds and Dick was dumbfounded, remaining sullenly silent for the rest of the day but his discrete evil eyes were kept focused on the rebel in the corner.

That evening, during his first bleak vigil in the bar, he sat alone at a table, a few yards away from several middle-aged bar flies who were stooped over the long bar. He nodded to them since they seemed to have been permanently ensconced there, in effect fixtures, since the major refurbishment years earlier.

Ralph knew them by sight but preferred the Friday lunch time sessions in the bar with a different clientele. Over several hours that evening a few customers drifted in and out, chatted to the barmaid, and then wandered off to new pubs.

It was spotting with rain, a miserable night, and there were not many revellers gracing the streets. Something told him Mark would not turn up and at closing time – 11pm – he went home, first glancing at the ageing mural of the little man riding a penny farthing, a quirky exit habit he had acquired over many years.

The following night he sat on the same stool at the same table, eyeing the door leading into the darkened back street. The bar flies tried to start a conversation since his second appearance in a week seemed to indicate he would be joining the cluster of has-beens on a semi-permanent basis. He politely ignored them and reverted to peering at the door and at the entrance to the barber's shop across the way, a shadowy place where he wondered whether his pal was standing out of sight in the darkness and keeping a wary eye on him.

Two more mute evening sit-ins were staged in the bar, at the end of which Ralph walked out without an iota of success, and he was beginning to believe that he was on the wrong trajectory, a futile enterprise fuelled by flawed judgement. Perhaps he did not know his friend after all.

Back at the office Dick was sombrely ruminating about his erratic reporter. Though Ralph continued to work office hours and carried out any engagements requested by his boss, his future was under review for insubordination, even though he was a long serving member of the staff who had caused little trouble in his 25-year career.

Chapter 25

The breakthrough came on a balmy evening. It was a Friday, and the bar was full of small groups of young people wedded to the traditional weekend pub crawl.

The door swung open and a man in a sports jacket, lightweight grey trousers and flat cap swept in, ignoring the regulars who were congregating near the pretty barmaid. Ralph looked up, for a moment not realising this intruder was the man himself. Mark removed his cap, smiled, and headed towards his onetime unofficial press officer, thrusting out his right hand in anticipation of a warm greeting. Ralph relaxed, grinned, and rose to greet him, ignoring the protruding hand and giving him a deep hug.

Mark bought a couple of drinks and despite that fact he had been the town's MP for nearly 15 years the huddle at the bar, fiercely debating the strengths and weaknesses of Northfield Rovers, the league team, ignored him. The duo moved to another table out of reach of prying eyes and ears and started talking about the old times. His disappearance, Janet and the Advertiser were never mentioned for a long time.

After half an hour more earnest issues started to filter into the conversation and the laughter, jokes, reminiscences, the old characters who had illuminated their early friendship started to dissipate and eventually Ralph asked the question: "What have you been up to? The last couple of years have been plain crazy."

Mark did not hesitate, explaining how he had evaded the legitimate aspects of governments and passport controls and how he had travelled between Australia and the UK, thanks to his friends in high places. Then he grumbled about his partner, Janet, whose sensational revelations in Joan's ribald newspaper were not that accurate. He wanted to put his version in a newspaper and the Advertiser was his choice. He realised the rest of the media would descend on the town like vultures following publication, but by that time he would enjoying his leisure in a police station.

"I have been hiding all over the place with friends and relatives in Northfield and I have not been out in the daylight. Even spent time in a cellar, like Joan. It was like living in the bunker at Two Trees. It's just got too much. All that isolation. It was just the same in Australia where I was equally terrified of being identified.

"Janet and I had a row, and I left. I am tired of being on the run. At first I did not trust you, particularly after the volatile bust-up in my house before I became a fugitive. Last night I spent an hour standing in a doorway across the way from this bar wondering whether to come in, and today I realised you are on my side on the grounds there was no sign of the law."

Mark became restive as a man well under the influence kept peering at him, his alcohol-infused mind desperately trying to identify the new man in the corner.

"Look," Mark declared. "I'll come to the office tomorrow. Don't mention it to anyone and I'll give you the full story and then the police station will be my subsequent destination. Okay. I'll ask for you in reception. Is Susan still there? Very nice young lady – fancied her every time I called in on a Friday to see you."

Ralph, now becoming nervous as well, had spotted the inquisitive drinker, too, and realised the man would soon come to his senses given that he knew Ralph from the old days when he was affectionately known as 'Scoop.'

He said: "Mark, you had better bolt before that guy's face lights up. You can see the cogs going round in his brain but now he's too befuddled even to order another drink. My identification will come to him tonight and yours will click once the hangover clears tomorrow."

"Before you go," he added, "who is in the grave 'down under', so to speak?"

Mark grinned: "Very droll, Ralph. My relatives over there are undertakers. The coffin is full of old books."

"Oh," he added. "I have forgotten to tell you. A

guy from Manchester is buying Two Trees. Never liked the place, really. My father lived in a modest house and on his way to work at the pit told his mates that was his favourite house, a palace. That's why I bought it. Misplaced nostalgia. After a couple of years it lost its appeal. The wife said she could hear eerie noises coming from rooms. I scared her stiff by saying that the old witch Mary Elliott had come back to weave her spells.

"My wife, who had seen a photograph of Mary in your newspaper a long time ago, was convinced she had seen the shadow of the old girl in the kitchen one evening. She could not sleep for weeks after that experience.

"There was something unusual about the place. One old guy said there were tales of spooky noises emanating from the house before our time. He was probably a drunk, but something must have happened. Strange."

"No problem with that one," Ralph replied. "It was an owl which took up residence when the place was empty. There were all kinds of fabricated stories after the war. The locals were fascinated by the links between Mary's early pristine respectability, then her potty behaviour and the later criminality - they kept her memory alive.

"Just think we are talking about her 40 years after her infamous court case. If you looked through our back numbers published in the 1940s, 50s and 60s you would see countless photographs of so-called local celebrities, civic leaders, MPs and businessmen.

Today no-one can name them, all have been forgotten. Not Mary. She's still talked about.

"People mention her generosity. Don said she owned lots of houses in Gorton and when she was convicted the tenants inundated the judge with letters praising her community spirit, her Christmas gifts and the fact that she had always kept rents at a minimum. She was a genuine lady bountiful. The Northfield Main Colliery Company and the prosecuting solicitors may not have thought so but the local residents did – they never forgot those food parcels handed out at Christmas in the middle of rationing. Probably some of the stuff came via the black market.

"She had another side to her personality of course. Young children in the village were kept quiet by being told ghost stories concocted by their older brothers or sisters on windy evenings, and guess which ones terrified them the most? The tales relating to our Mary. I reckon her presence is still felt at Two Trees which she loved dearly."

Both laughed and Mark added: "If she is hanging around the house in spirit, she'll soon be on her way. The new owner is to demolish the house and build another on the site. He's filling in the tunnels because he's scared someone from the Ministry is going to turn up and say they should be kept for posterity, a reminder about the grim days during the war.

"As per usual, I'll give you a little gem at the end. Did you know Dr Potter, the previous owner of the house? Well, it seems his wife has been fined in the south for shoplifting. Do you think the house attracted the criminal classes or do you think nice people were drawn to a sinister house and then changed into baddies?"

He leaned back and laughed again. The outburst made the cogs whir again in the mind of the inquisitive drinker sitting at the bar but the identity of the man with the vaguely familiar face remained a mystery.

What an exclusive, Ralph concluded on the way home, though he thought the remark about the relatives being undertakers may have been a figment of Mark's imagination. A free scoop as well, for Mark had never mentioned money unlike his avaricious partner in Australia. He turned the key in the front door, switched on the light in the kitchen and made a late-night cup of tea. What surprised him was that he wasn't that enthusiastic about the story. That combination of excitement and angst that came with a big one wasn't there anymore.

As for Mark? The great escape had left his moon face drawn and perhaps haggard, his grey hair was receding badly, and Ralph had detected the beginnings of a stoop. Time had given him a mauling and Ralph was not surprised the heavy drinkers in the bar had not recognised him.

Mark was punctual as usual. Striding into reception as if it was a normal day in the not-too-distant past, he smiled at Susan, whom he had always admired from afar. She slumped in her chair at first sight and nearly had a breakdown since like almost everyone else she thought he was dead.

"You know who I want, Susan," he said with his habitual wink. "I'll sit down and wait."

Her internal phone call to the editorial department had Ralph hurrying down the flight of stairs and into reception.

"Wait until you see my boss's face," said Ralph, grinning like the proverbial cat. "I am going to enjoy this more than anything else. I am even enjoying being a devious person, kicking over the traces and all that. Come on let the pandemonium begin."

The duo walked into the editorial room and the typewriters ceased chattering. One or two of the reporters recognised the errant MP immediately but not Dick, a newcomer to Northfield, who was mildly myopic and who was distracted by other matters.

"Who is this person?" he asked, glaring at Ralph. He did not give the politician a second glance. "Why have you brought him here? Is this one of your deadbeat contacts in the taproom? I do not appreciate a joke like this."

"Really? This is not a joke," replied Ralph, now pumped up with the knowledge that he had the boss on the run.

"This is Mark Pinder, runaway MP. You do not recognise him because you are not a local man and because you have not looked at him properly. Right. I am going. Dick, you haven't done any work for two days. Unless, of course, the occasional glare at me across the office is deemed work by you. So, I'll let you write the story and take the glory. You'll find

Mark won't hurt you and he's an amenable character. You'll be able to dine off this story for six months.

"Superb, suuuu-per. Cheerio," he concluded, mocking Dick's favourite words.

"Where are you going?" asked Dick, first angry and now beginning to tremble with the burden that he was carrying. He would have to make a good job of the interview and the writing, or he would become the office joke.

"I am the one who says who does what. This is your job, not mine."

"Not today, it isn't," came the reply. "You are writing it up. It will do you good. You'll appreciate the efforts of the deadbeats in the office in the future. Don't wait up; I do not think I'll be coming back today. Things to do, what-a-to-do.

"Oh, I think I'm going to get another visitor but first I am going out to have a cup of coffee," added Ralph. "By the way, I hope you appreciate the origins and significance of this story. You do not find this kind of thing at the town hall or at the Rotary Club. It's all down to building up contacts over many years, winning their confidence and knowing when and where to have a pint on a muggy night in Northfield."

Mark, embarrassed by the diatribe, wanted to change the subject, peering hard at Dick's desk: "Is that the love desk? Where all the action took place years ago? Look - the polished top appears to have ageing spots. Or are they skid marks? It looks like it had plenty of fornication in its day."

A couple of the older reporters giggled into their

hands, but Dick did not know what was happening, still confused by Ralph's decision to abandon the job for the day. He had never heard the old stories about the staff's quickies on the desk.

"What fornication? What kind of action? What's been going on for years? If that has been used for merriment and sexual adventure, then I'll get rid of it. It's not staying in here."

"That's the one," replied Ralph, smiling. "Never used it; we had the comfort of a flat. That reminds me, Mark – I think she'll be arriving tomorrow, the delightful and delectable Joan. Better prepare my plans for sweet revenge."

Chapter 26

The following day Dick, having splashed the story all over the front page, was euphoric and fawned over Ralph, whom he now regarded as a kind of prodigal brother. Everyone was so excited about the story they turned in on a Saturday to deal with phone calls and handle the national newspaper lads who were laying siege to the office.

Welcoming the saccharine attention of the media, Dick believed his place in the roll of honour among journalists was now assured; no longer was he a second-rate Editor in charge of the local rag.

"Superb, suuuu-per," he muttered to himself, first making sure Ralph was not within earshot.

Joan was pumped-up, ready for a bloody encounter with her ex. After booking into a country house hotel in the Peak District, she arrived in Northfield, having received a thunderous telling -off from her boss who wanted to know why she had not known about the Advertiser's exclusive. She managed to squeeze her expensive sports car into the office car park.

Ralph was working well and having returned from yet another coffee break – taken without permission - he found a quarrelsome Joan waiting in reception. Susan, the receptionist, was in a chaotic mood, wondering what was going to happen next since she had not seen the well-groomed visitor for years. First Mark Pinder now Joan, the flamboyant darling of the swinging 1960s, and Susan smiled at her fading memory of the fresh-faced young reporter striding down the corridor in a mini skirt.

Meanwhile, upstairs, yet another posse of hacks grilled Dick, who was sporting a new suit as he once again recounted the startling interview with back-from-the grave Mark. The more he went over the story the more exaggerated it became.

"Come on," Ralph told Joan. "Let's get out of here. I'll take you down to The Penny Farthing for an early drink. That's what you usually do, isn't it? An early cocktail in London to pep-up the day?"

"No cracks, Ralph; I'm not in the mood. What's happening? I have read the Advertiser's big exclusive on Mark. There must be more. More titillating stuff. Why wasn't I told what the newspaper was planning? I can't trust you anymore. Why wasn't your by-line on the story?"

"Are you kidding?" he replied. "Since when you have been a custodian of the truth, trust and friendship. Come on, let's go."

In the bar, Joan, gazing around in boredom, could not understand what she ever saw in the place, with its flock wallpaper and a mural that failed miserably to reprise the atmosphere in a smart London pub. A misspent youth was the problem, she thought to herself, and in this case the youth was Ralph in the old days.

"This hotel doesn't change," she moaned, eyeing Ralph across the table.

"Oh, you'll like this story. Janet has disappeared in Australia, taken off with some of my money. I was bewitched with the story and did not realise what was happening. My own money. What was left of our holiday fund. She wanted an advance to pay bills, she claimed. Ran off with a man from down the road."

Ralph stifled a grin but did not say anything.

"Right," she demanded, "what's happening here? I do not have all day, what about you? I have been told Dick, the new Donald Duck in the office, doesn't like you. After we have finished you'll need to rush back to the office to see the new daddy to calm you down."

"Books," he replied, having decided not to get over serious; he wanted to turn the rest of the afternoon into a wizard session of jokes and ambiguities designed to fox his old love.

"Books? What's that mean?"

"That's what the police in Australia will find when exhuming Mark's grave. A coffin full of books."

"How do you know that? That wasn't mentioned in the Advertiser's story."

"I am not messing about, Ralph? Where is he? The Scarlet Pimpernel. I seek him here; I seek him there, the elusive Pindernel. You see, I have read a few books in my time. Do you recall The Scarlet

Pimpernel?"

"A little contrived," added Ralph, smiling, "I think you are trying too hard to produce snappy words. As for Mark he's at the police station. After the interview with Dick, he went to give himself up. Like a good citizen. Even now I am unsure whether he's done anything unlawful, so he'll probably be walking down Market Hill by now and trying to dodge his former mates, the miners.

"The Labour Party will boot him out and select a new candidate to take his place and the House of Commons' standards committee will want to grill him."

She was not interested in his comments.

"He must have told you something more. You wouldn't have told Dick everything you know. You are holding something back. What is it?"

"No comment."

"What do you mean 'no comment'?"

"No comment."

"Stop fooling."

"You have heard the words before. From your celebrity friends. You know what it means."

"I am going, getting out of this place," she said, sharply. "Are you coming?"

"No thanks," he said, pushing his multi-coloured cocktail to the other side of the table, and adding: "I am going to order a pint of bitter. More my style. That's what you once said: I was a bit of rough who liked grubby pints of beer."

"I can't recall saying that. What are you going to

do? I am still waiting. Have I just wasted thousands of pounds on a holiday in Australia? My bank account has been plundered over the past month, you know, and you were one of the raiders. Have I blown all that money for nothing? You have had a free holiday down under; surely you owe me? I was hoping to patch things up with you. Can't we settle our grievances?"

She broke off the lecture to peer at him in astonishment, pointing to his wild mop of hair before laughing.

"What's wrong?" he queried, ill at ease for the first time that day.

"You are going grey – Ralph, you are getting old. Good grief. Grey. What will your mother say? Or Don for that matter? Oh, dear, I have forgotten – he's dead, isn't he?"

She shook with merriment, momentarily forgetting about the MP and looking human for the first time in weeks. He warbled on, though his confidence was beginning to ebb since he didn't relish becoming old. He changed the subject and turned serious.

"I am going to walk outside, sit at one of the tables in the back street and indulge in a spot of nostalgia. I am going to recall some of the old miners, their humour and the camaraderie that made life tolerable underground. A rare breed of men – gone too soon. Very sad.

"I'm tired of newspapers and tired of life, love."

Her face hardened at the sound of the word 'love'

but she did not say anything since she was losing the verbal battle.

Pointing to the old mural of the top-hatted little man in a dark suit and top hat pedalling madly on the penny farthing, he said: "I feel like him. Working hard for years and not getting anywhere while others in my life streak past on gleaming new bikes without any effort."

Unimpressed and viewing the mural with disdain, she said: "I thought it was Peter the bike man's grandfather delivering goodies in the Victorian era."

Ignoring her, he continued: "All those years I spent assiduously building a list of good contacts in the National Union of Mineworkers and the National Coal Board. All of them kept me in stories for 20 years.

"They were all superb during the miners' strike in 1984/85. Then they lost their jobs. A magnificent industry collapsed and vanished and I was left with zilch, too old to start developing contacts again in another industry or at that wretched town hall. Like the miners, I was in a way out of a job.

"One of the minor things I learned from our holiday in Australia is that I need adventure. Spent too much time in this town. So, I am going elsewhere, and I have no idea what I am going to do. Freedom at last. It's something I should have done in the 1960s when life was supposed to swing with Marianne Faithful and sunflowers but didn't."

Joan gave him a withering look, turned, and

strode out of the bar, ramrod-straight and unimpeachably self-assured and untouched by all his rhetoric. She headed down the narrow back street and never looked back until reaching the junction with the main road.

She halted, turned, and peered at the lonely figure sipping beer at the table outside the bar. She saw adorable weakness, felt sorry for him and went for the jugular.

"I have forgotten to tell you about my guilty secret," she shouted. "I have to get it off my chest."

"What is it?" came a petulant reply.

"Your pal, Peter, the pedal man who pedelled sex and Persil and Lifebuoy soap to the ladies on groovy estates. He once gave me a tender sweet kiss in a backyard. Years ago, mind you. It was so magical I became melancholic and besotted. The trouble is he would not start until I had told him my mother's Northfield Co-operative Society's divi number. 95304."

"That's awful," he responded, almost grief-stricken. "Wait until I see him, the cheeky sod. I'll punch him on the chin. Just a minute. Come on, you are kidding? Aren't you?"

"Of course, darling, what made you think we shopped at the dreadful Co-op? I just made up that divi number. But he wasn't bad looking. It might have really happened under different circumstances. I wonder whether he asked his Jezebels for their divi numbers before giving them a decent rogering?"

"Well, are you coming?" she continued, abruptly

changing the subject. "You are no longer handcuffed to the town through your job or to Don in the office. Hurry up, we do not have all day. I promise you an adventure-a-day in London, unexpurgated at that."

"You are 50 paces away," he shouted back, hoarsely. "We can't communicate like that. I can hardly hear you. Those blokes waiting their turn in the barbers across the way are giving us funny looks and laughing – it's their only drama of the day. Aren't you going after Mark, he must be free by now?"

"No, darling. I am giving up on the fast life. It's not worth it. Handing in my notice today and Mark can go to hell. Just decided. Impulsive, aren't I? I have had a light bulb experience. No; the floodlights have been turned on in my mind. Never realised my life so far has been so empty. Glamorous but hollow. A self-inflicted glitzy scam.

"The job became part of my personality. It wasn't just the kidnapping that turned me nasty at times. So did the job. Now I'm turning my back on the lot. I haven't got anything meaningful – except you. I never realised that until I saw you drinking by yourself at that table.

"Loved you all along. There are times when I cannot get your looks out of my mind. Even when writing a story: one afternoon I typed Ralph Caine rather than Michael Caine and the sub editor went mad. Are you going to get your posterior off that chair?"

The lads in the barbers opened the door with glee, listening intently to the amorous misadventure unfurling before them, urging him to pursue his sweetheart. Elderly shoppers standing in the street tuned into the couple's loud exchanges as well, transfixed by what they saw as a modern romance with all its allied tribulations.

"Go on, mate," shouted one of his pals sitting in the barbers, "go after her. Tie the knot like the rest of us and be miserable for the rest of your life. Get your wedding pictures in the Advertiser next week -Ralph, you'll look good in white."

"Come on Ralph, Catch Me If You Can," she shouted into the cool late afternoon air: the words trailed down the street, taunting him. Realising he was on the verge of capitulation, she stoked-up more bawdy entertainment and the lads in Baxter's barbers waved back in appreciation.

"Don't forget to bring your heavy pit boots, Ralph – they'll add spice in the bedroom," she quipped, playing to her wide-eyed audience. "You can wear the trousers, and I'll put on the boots. You'll be able to make love without forgetting your roots in mining."

The wags in the barbers, now scenting blood and the prospect of further outrageous humour, roared with laughter, the sound of which could be heard at the town hall at the top of the hill. Unsatiated, they demanded more, and the lovers responded, one laughing while the other was seemingly enmeshed in a kind of male nightmare.

Drat it, he thought. What is she going to say next? This is highly embarrassing. That lot in the barber's shop think this is a kind of pantomime. Half an hour ago I was on top. Now's she's winning all the way. Another defeat.

"I am coming, love, just finishing my beer…"

"Don't call me 'love'! It's working class and provincial, darling. Hurry up."

She fired back: "I thought you were tired of me?"

"My impetuosity and my impudicity have changed my mind," he added, hoping that two Advertiser-banned long words would befuddle the audience, most of whom were loyal fans of the newspaper. Instead, they became more excitable.

"Life in London sounds like a good proposition," he announced, having no longer the stamina to continue fighting. "Nothing here anymore."

He added: "I am doing a Derek Lee and walking away from this town."

She frowned: "What on earth are you talking about? Who is Derek Lee? Another Victor what's-his-name, the absentee MP? You are spitting out riddles."

"Forget it," he replied laughing - he had won one.

He rose slowly, reminiscent of a sombre Don rising awkwardly from his old chair with a sheet of copy paper in his hand, a signal he was on his way to give an unfortunate reporter a rollicking for making a factual error or for writing a cliché.

As he strolled towards her, swaying a little as the early morning drink took effect and with the cheering of his pals in the barbers urging him on, she smiled and felt at ease.

Drinkers who rarely left their seats in an afternoon in the Penny Farthing were alerted by the uncustomary racket in the back street and appeared at the dusty windows, peering silently, woozily and enviously as the bar's escapee headed down the pavement. The smart money -when they managed to get their brains in gear - was on a forthcoming marriage.

There was a chorus of cheers and hoots as the couple hugged, kissed and strolled towards the office car park without glancing behind them. Grinning, Ralph thought at that kind of moment in an old film 'The End' would have appeared on their backs.

It wasn't the end, however. On entering the car park, they froze, and Ralph nearly wept at what confronted them. Four workmen were placing tarpaulin over Don's desk which was positioned on a flat-back lorry ready for the antique dealer's auction room.

"Oh, dear," he said, his face dropping. "That's it. Must be the end of the newspaper. Don said that once the desk went that would be it. The end of writing about the council as we know it."

He went on: "I have not told anyone this before. If he thought no-one was watching, he would stroke the fine mahogany as if it was a woman and smile to himself, after which he would turn into the doom-laden boss again. Kept everything neat and tidy on that desk – his typewriter was a well-oiled machine, too – and he never slammed the drawers when stressed like the latest boss."

Joan thrust her elbow into his ribs: "Do not be silly, love. Cheer up. "

He gave her a funny look on hearing 'love' but remained quiet as he recalled her facial slaps. Perhaps, just perhaps, the wonderful Yorkshire word 'thee' would eventually infiltrate her otherwise impeccable vocabulary, he thought. That would be a grand day. He did not say anything but chuckled at the thought; she returned the funny look.

Having failed to realise the dreaded L-word word had been uttered, she continued: "It's just a desk with a shady past. Come on quick, let's get into my car and be off. Leave this lot behind. The whole industry is careering towards oblivion, but we are getting out. We are on the run like Mark. Marvellous, isn't it? Kicking over the traces again, nothing like it."

They were determined to have a go at settling down before it was too late. It was worth a gamble and the future was a far-off country. No more quarrelling; no more bleak and lengthy separations.

On their way south in her blue Ferrari 166 she said: "Nice motor, isn't it, darling. 1950 model. Do you like it? Fast car, fast lady?"

"Nope. It stands out like a sore thumb – the police will chase you down the road in this one, they'll enjoy booking you."

Disregarding his reply and the 'sore thumb' cliché, she continued: "When we settle in and I've given up work, I'm going to do a spot of painting. Always fancied being an artist. What are you going to do? Gardening? No, I do not think I can see you doing that. Well?"

"Nope," he replied, straight faced. "Look for Victor."

"Victor? Victor who? Who the hell is Victor? Oh, no, you are not going to search for that missing MP from the 1920s, are you? Ralph he's dead, no one cares anymore. You are driving me nuts again. No, darling don't do this to me. Not now. Anything but Victor.

"Seriously you are just about daft enough to go looking for bloody Victor. I thought we were going to be like normal people. Cooking, gardening, perhaps a family. Not behaving like a grave digger searching for a corpse."

"It's one of the great mysteries of my dad's time," he replied, stifling a grin. "It can be solved even now. The authorities have not asked the correct questions in the past. Was he spying for the Russians or the IRA? What do you think, darling?"

Sensing a wind-up, she accelerated: "I always wanted to do this to you but my dream of giving you a fright on the A-1 was brutally interrupted by my incarceration underground all those years ago. Do you remember? We were going to have a naughty weekend in London, and I was going to drive like a bat out of hell. Hold on to your greying hair."

The speedometer needle rose sharply and hovered perilously around 90mph; Ralph froze: "I think I overacted there, darling, can't we slow down?"

"Nope!!! Gosh!!! we are in a hurry to find jolly old Victor…remember, luvvie?"

Ralph's eyes opened wide: "Joan, Joan! I have something to say."

"Well go on. What is it? Another cliché on your part?"

"Yes."

He shouted: "I love you! I love you!"

"And I love you too…"

THE END

Murder, Scandal and Cliches

Printed in Dunstable, United Kingdom